"Damn 〈...〉 ting

"I couldn't for〈...〉 you," he said softly. "That *would* be the impossible dream. But I had managed to stop thinking of what might have been. And then you drove up this afternoon, and it was like you'd never left."

Rebecca's throat ached. His name was more a gasp than a whisper as she flung her arms around him and buried her face in the crook of his shoulder. "I never meant to hurt you."

"You couldn't help my falling in love with you. Even I couldn't have prevented that. It was as inevitable as the sun rising in the east."

"I'm not the right woman for you, Roth."

"I love you. That makes you the right woman."

She pulled away. "We want different things. Sooner or later we'd hurt each other."

"Why is that high rise so important to you, Rebecca? What would you have there that you couldn't have with me?"

"A view," she said breathlessly. "A view alive with people."

Dear Reader,

Although our culture is always changing, the desire to love and be loved is a constant in every woman's heart. Silhouette Romances reflect that desire, sweeping you away with books that will make you laugh and cry, poignant stories that will move you time and time again.

This year we're featuring Romances with a playful twist. Remember those fun-loving heroines who always manage to get themselves into tricky predicaments? You'll enjoy reading about their escapades in Silhouette Romances by Brittany Young, Debbie Macomber, Annette Broadrick and Rita Rainville.

We're also publishing Romances by many of your all-time favorites such as Ginna Gray, Diana Palmer and Joan Hohl. Your overwhelming reaction to these authors has served as a touchstone for us, and we're pleased to bring you more books with Silhouette's distinctive medley of charm, wit and—above all—*romance*. I hope you enjoy this book, and the many stories to come.

Sincerely,

Rosalind Noonan
Senior Editor
SILHOUETTE BOOKS

GLENDA SANDS
Amended Dreams

Published by Silhouette Books New York

America's Publisher of Contemporary Romance

SILHOUETTE BOOKS
300 E. 42nd St., New York, N.Y. 10017

Copyright © 1986 by Glenda Sands

All rights reserved, including the right to reproduce
this book or portions thereof in any form whatsoever.
For information address Silhouette Books,
300 E. 42nd St., New York, N.Y. 10017

ISBN: 0-373-08447-1

First Silhouette Books printing July 1986

All the characters in this book are fictitious. Any
resemblance to actual persons, living or dead, is
purely coincidental.

SILHOUETTE, SILHOUETTE ROMANCE and colophon
are registered trademarks of the publisher.

America's Publisher of Contemporary Romance

Printed in the U.S.A.

Books by Glenda Sands

Silhouette Romance

The Mockingbird Suite #337
A Taste of Romance #389
Heart Shift #409
Tall, Dark and Handsome #434
Amended Dreams #447

GLENDA SANDS

is a Houston writer who, upon finding eighteen growing chicks taking up residence in her daughter's bedroom, threw up her hands and said, "There's got to be a book in this!"

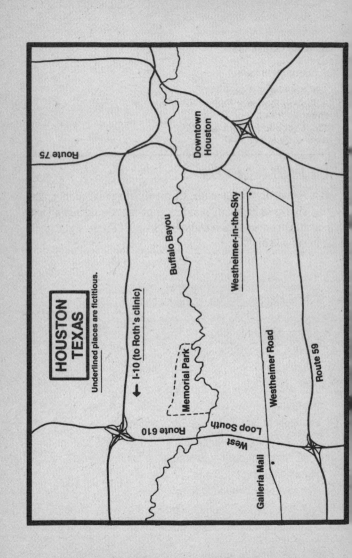

HOUSTON
TEXAS

Underlined places are fictitious.

← I-10 (to Roth's clinic)

Route 75

Downtown
Houston

Westheimer-in-the-Sky

Buffalo Bayou

Memorial Park

Westheimer Road

Route 59

Route 610

West
Loop South

Galleria Mall

Chapter One

I don't want a man to come and take Elvira away,"
said Lisa. Her attitude was petulant, but Rebecca
Bruner noted the telltale quiver of her niece's lips as
the little girl spoke.

"Neither do I," Kevin piped up. "Elvira belongs
to us."

Rebecca resisted the very human urge to strangle
the two of them and wondered if being a parent was
as fraught with no-win situations as was being an
aunt. "You can't have a pet turkey," she said.
"We've discussed it, remember? There's no place to
keep Elvira."

"She likes the bathtub," argued Lisa.

"The bathtub in an apartment is no place for a
turkey," Rebecca said, not for the first time. She re-

peated other previously pleaded arguments. "Soon she'll be too big for the bathtub, and she'd be scratching at the carpets. Only cats are allowed in this complex, anyway."

Kevin shot her a ten-year-old's look of defiance. "We have a yard at home. We can take Elvira when Mommy and Daddy come back."

"Elvira wouldn't stay in a yard, either," Rebecca said wearily. "And there are deed restrictions against fowl in your neighborhood."

"Mommy could go to court and make the judge let us have Elvira," Lisa said.

Rebecca rolled her eyes heavenward. How long could this go on? "Your mommy doesn't want a turkey any more than I do," she said sharply. "Now you two go say goodbye to Elvira while I get dinner started."

The dam within Lisa broke. "I don't want Elvira to go away," she wailed, her tears giving way to heart-rending sobs. Rebecca comforted the child, glad that she had changed out of her dry-clean-only suit into jeans as her niece's tears saturated the poly-cotton of her shirt.

Losing Elvira was only a minuscule part of what was bothering Lisa, Rebecca knew. The seven-year-old was missing her parents and the neighborhood children, feeling stifled by the constricting atmosphere of apartment living at her aunt's, and coping with the loss of a grandparent.

And that, thought Rebecca, was a lot for a seven-year-old to handle. Rebecca was twenty-six and having a bit of a problem handling everything herself. If she didn't feel the responsibility to remain the composed adult in front of her niece and nephew, she'd enjoy a good cry herself. In fact, she might just indulge herself in one as soon as the kids were in bed. She was close to exploding, and would prefer to let go in the privacy of her own bedroom rather than breaking down at work over some minor frustration. That would be intolerable.

At last Lisa heaved a final releasing sob and drew away from her aunt, sniffing solemnly. "Feel better?" Rebecca asked.

Lisa shook her head. "I'm still sad."

"Let's go wash your face. You'll feel better afterward."

"I'll have to say good...bye to Cheeper and Peeper and Tail Feathers, too," Lisa said as Rebecca swept the washcloth over her face.

"That's a good idea," replied Rebecca, relieved that the child had accepted the inevitability of losing the chicks and the turkey.

"I'll miss them," Lisa said.

"Of course you will," Rebecca said. "But they'll have a good home. This man said he had a nice pen for them, with a separate pen for Elvira."

"What's his name?" interjected Kevin, who had been eavesdropping in the open doorway.

"Roth." Rebecca answered. "Mr. Roth."

"Is he a nice man?" Kevin asked skeptically.

"He sounded nice on the telephone," Rebecca said.

When both children were engrossed in playing with Elvira and the dozen and a half chicken biddies in the bathroom, Rebecca stole away to the kitchen and began trimming the fat from the edges of the chops she'd planned for dinner. When the doorbell rang, she wiped her hands and went to open the door, noticing Lisa and Kevin lurking in the shadows of the hallway to check out the man who'd come for their beloved pets.

The nice telephone voice of Lawrence Roth turned out to be connected to a rather stunning, solidly built man. He was just over six feet tall with curly brown hair and startling blue eyes that appraised her curiously but not suggestively. "Ms. Bruner?"

She smiled and extended her hand, hoping it wasn't still greasy from the pork chops. "Would you like to look at the chicks before we box them up?"

"That won't be necessary. The ad said they were healthy."

"Rhode Island Red pullets," she said. "And, of course, the Bourbon Red turkey hen."

Lisa took a tentative step into the living room and said in a tiny voice, "Her name is Elvira."

Roth regarded her carefully. "Whose name is Elvira, honey?"

"The turkey's," she said as though the question were ridiculous.

He looked from her to Rebecca, and a frown wrinkled his brow. "I see," he said slowly, a note of censure in his voice that Rebecca couldn't quite understand.

"We haven't named all the chicks," volunteered Lisa, and the frown on Roth's face deepened.

"Why don't you and Kevin go get the chicks in their box," Rebecca suggested. Then, turning to Roth, she said, "I'm afraid the children have gotten rather attached to them."

"Obviously," Roth said sharply. "Tell me, did you dye them with food coloring? Are they pink and yellow and blue?"

Rebecca blinked in incomprehension. "Why would I do anything so preposterous?"

"Isn't that the standard procedure with Easter chicks? Did you give any thought before you bought the chicks to what you would do with them after the novelty wore off? Or did you think they'd die of overhandling before they became a problem?"

She found his audacity infuriating. "Now just a moment, Mr. Roth. You've got the situation all wrong."

He cocked an irritated eyebrow. "Dr. Roth," he corrected. "Doctor of veterinary medicine. And I don't believe I do. I've seen this type of thing again and again. You don't have the facilities for pets, but you brought them home so the kids could enjoy them, with no consideration for the animals themselves."

Something snapped inside Rebecca at his unjust accusation; it was the last straw. Suddenly, the load she was carrying became too heavy to bear.

"That's not the case here, *Doctor* Roth," she said scathingly, her eyes burning with tears that could no longer be contained. "You don't know what you're talking about. I bought those chicks for my father, and I'm not the least bit sorry I did because he died happy, knowing there were chicks in the henhouse." She snuffled loudly. "And they haven't been mishandled, as you seem to think, because I showed Lisa and Kevin how to be gentle with them. One reason they're so attached to them is that they're missing their parents because my sister stayed behind at the farm to settle the estate. Furthermore, you don't know what it's been like trying to play mother and driving across town in the morning rush-hour traffic to take them to school, and worrying about the apartment manager evicting me because this is an adults-only complex and my neighbors are complaining about the noise the kids make in the halls, and hoping she doesn't find out about the chickens and that stupid turkey because she really would evict me then."

She sniffed mightily again. "I tried to find a home for them before I left the farm, I really did, but I couldn't." She was crying in earnest now and might have felt sorry for Roth if she'd been calm enough to notice the look of helplessness on his face. She wiped her cheek with the back of her hand and went on with her tirade. "And what's more, I happen to be an active member of Citizens for Animal Protection, and I stuff envelopes with letters urging people to be responsible pet owners and have their animals neutered, and I even clean cages in the CAP showroom sometimes. So don't lecture me about not caring about animals."

As she burst into a fresh torrent of tears, she found herself crying against a sturdy shoulder, reassuring in its solidity and cozy in its masculine warmth and woodsy after-shave scent. Large, devastatingly gentle hands were stroking her back, and the voice of her accuser was soothing as it spoke reassuringly in her ear. "It's okay. It'll be all right. No one thinks you did anything wrong. Of course it's been tough on you."

The hands continued to soothe her with tender strokes, the voice crooned softly on and on, and gradually her sobs subsided until she was just snuffling quietly in the haven of his arms. Awareness returned to her slowly and she lifted her head, embarrassed. Kevin and Lisa were staring at her, mesmerized and a little apprehensive.

Wiping her cheeks with her fingertips, she sniffed and cleared her throat, preparing to speak to them. But Dr. Roth spoke instead. "Your aunt needs a tissue. Can you find her one?"

The children looked to Rebecca for confirmation, and she nodded her head as she sank onto the sofa. They returned quickly, mission accomplished. Rebecca pulled a tissue from the box and mumbled a thank-you.

"Are you all right, Aunt Becca?" Lisa patted her arm.

Rebecca covered the child's hand with her own. "Yes, Lisa. I'm better now."

She turned to Dr. Roth, who was standing nearby, flexing his hands nervously. "I'm sorry for that outburst," she said. "It's been a rough couple of weeks. I guess I was primed to explode."

"I'm the one who needs to apologize. I went leaping to a lot of wrong conclusions. You had enough pressure on you without some zealot for animal welfare hurling accusations at you."

"Your shirt!" she cried, appalled at the large wet stain. "I'll rinse it out for you. I've got a dryer."

He shrugged. "It's nothing really. A bit of salt water. It'll air-dry in a few minutes." He smiled away the objection she was about to make. "A veterinarian gets much worse from his patients."

She forced a smile for the children. "See, kids?" she said to them. "Dr. Roth is an animal doctor. Elvira and the chicks couldn't be getting a better home." Turning back to him she said, "I guess you're anxious to be on your way. I'll go see if the chicks are boxed up and ready to go."

She got up and started toward the bathroom, but he stopped her. "I have a better idea." He tilted his head toward the raw meat on the counter. "Is that your dinner?"

"Y-yes."

"You're in no shape to cook. I'd say you deserve a night off kitchen duty. Why don't we go out for a pizza?"

Flustered, Rebecca said, "We couldn't possibly impose..."

"No imposition," he insisted. "I'm a pizza-holic."

"But—"

"After all, you're giving me a dozen and a half Rhode Island Reds and a Bourbon Red turkey hen. It's the least I could do."

"I don't think—"

"Let's ask the kids," he said. He turned to Lisa and Kevin. "How would you guys like to go out for pizza? I think I saw a Showbiz on my way here."

The children reacted instantly, squealing in unison, "Showbiz!" Lisa gripped Rebecca's hand. "We can go, can't we, Aunt Becca? Please?"

"Lisa, I'm afraid..."

Roth half grinned, half gloated over his victory, then leaned close enough to speak to her without the children overhearing. "It's perfectly all right. I'm a good driver, an upstanding citizen and a former Boy Scout."

And a very irritating man who's obviously accustomed to getting his own way, she thought.

Lisa pulled at Rebecca's hand again. "Please," she begged, and Kevin joined his sister in a chorus of

"Please...? Please...? Please?" until Rebecca threw up her hands in surrender.

"Okay!" she said, glaring at Roth. "You two go wash your hands. With soap."

"I want to say," she told Roth when the children had left the room, "that I'll get even for this, but I can't imagine how."

"Why don't you just wrap up that meat and enjoy an evening out?"

"You're very presumptuous, Dr. Roth."

His blue eyes narrowed as he considered her remark. "There are times when all of us need to have someone else take charge and force us to do what's good for us."

Rebecca closed her eyes and sighed, letting her hand rest limply on the counter next to the meat. When she opened them, she said, "And you think Showbiz Pizza is the proper prescription for me?"

"I'd make the prescription a bit more generic—a change of scenery, some diversion from routine, a little relaxation. Showbiz fits in this instance."

Having put the meat away in the refrigerator, Rebecca closed the door and smiled at him sheepishly. "You may be right, Dr. Roth."

"Such a lovely smile proves it."

She raised a skeptical eyebrow. "Is such blatant blarney part of the prescription?"

"That was no blarney, Ms. Bruner, it was a sincere compliment."

Chapter Two

The pizza parlor reverberated with the clamor of merrymaking and electronic games. After ordering at the front window, Dr. Roth divided a handful of game tokens between Kevin and Lisa, and the two were off to toss skeeballs and defend planet Earth against alien invaders. He and Rebecca retreated to a table in a distant corner, close enough to keep an eye on the children, but far enough away from the sizzle of disintegrating aliens to permit conversation.

Roth leaned casually against the wall, his arms crossed. The spot on his shirt had dried without leaving a mark, and Rebecca thought idly that he looked like one of those people who could survive a blueberry pie fight without getting a stain on a white suit.

"It was pure luck finding your ad," he said. "I was planning on buying some chicks this week."

"You said you live just outside of town?"

"I have a few acres of what used to be a dairy farm out toward Katy. There's a chicken yard, but I just got around to making some necessary repairs last weekend."

In a purely professional reflex, Rebecca calculated the approximate value of land in the area he had mentioned. It was substantial: multiacre tracts in that area were prime targets for developers. Her curiosity piqued, she asked, "Have you been there long?"

"Less than a year. For a while I commuted into town for my practice, but I was able to set up a clinic next to the house in January."

"I see," said Rebecca, a bit disappointed. What had she expected—a detailed explanation of how he had come to own the property?

Roth readjusted his shoulders against the wall. "Tell me about the chicks—you bought them for your father, and he ... Is it too soon for you to talk about it?"

She smiled wryly. "You mean, can I talk about it without getting hysterical? Yes. All that before was a combination of circumstances. I promise not to create any scenes in public."

He opened his mouth to say something gallant, noticed that she was smiling and responded with a friendly, almost boyish grin. He liked a woman who could laugh at herself.

"His death was not unexpected," she began. "He was in his seventies, and he'd been in poor health for some time. We—my sister and her family and I— went up for Easter."

She took a breath to steel herself before continuing. "It's been a couple of years since he was able to keep any large animals on the farm, but he's always had chickens and raised a turkey for Thanksgiving. When we got there, he seemed so...des pondent...over the fact that his chickens had died off that I went out and bought the chicks. Over my sister's vehement objections, I might add. As usual, she was the cool, detached voice of logic. She's an attorney, and quite a formidable adversary, but I just ignored her."

Rebecca's eyes grew moist. "Dad was like a kid with a new bicycle. He carried the boxes out to the hutch and strung up a light for warmth, and fixed the food and water just so. He was slow, but he didn't want any help. He puttered with it for over an hour. I'll never forget the look on his face when he came back to the house." She looked directly at Roth. "He died in his sleep. A peaceful death."

There was a pause in the conversation, punctuated by zaps, zings and whoops from the electronic game machines.

After a respectable interval, Roth asked, "Where did he live?"

"In east Texas, in the middle of nowhere, near a spot in the road called Deadwood."

"So the Ms. Bruner of Land-Com Realty is a farm girl from east Texas."

Rebecca stiffened. Had the diction exercises, the books she'd read, all the hard work on her career been for naught? Underneath it all, was she still plain little Becky Bruner, farm girl? Hadn't the nice clothes, the sleek hairstyle, the manicured nails, the professional success transformed her? Or was she merely playing a role pretending to be the cosmopolitan sophisticate?

With that simple statement, he had succinctly voiced all her self-doubts. *So the Ms. Bruner of Land-Com Realty is a farm girl from east Texas.* She'd come a long way from Deadwood, but had she gotten anywhere? Sometimes she felt as though she were running in place.

Roth knew he'd struck a nerve but was unsure what he'd said to trigger such a dramatic response in her. She had actually grown pale. A delayed reaction to talking about her father's death? He didn't think so. It was something else, something different. She recovered quickly and was about to say something when Lisa approached and announced, "Aunt Becca, we're ready to clobber the gopher."

"You're ready to what?" Rebecca asked.

"Come *on*," Lisa insisted, pulling her by the hand. "Kevin's waiting."

"Maybe we'd better follow," said Roth, putting his hand on Rebecca's elbow. "Clobbering gophers sounds like serious business."

Kevin was hanging impatiently on the edge of a metal box that was just slightly taller than an adult's waist level, holding a club that was attached to the box by a cord. The weapon looked menacing, but it could not have been as heavy as it appeared because Kevin was obviously having no difficulty in lifting it. Upon spying them, he excitedly admonished them to hurry, his entire body vibrating with that excitement exclusive to childhood.

Without further preamble, he handed the club to Roth. After giving Rebecca a conspiratorial wink, the doctor turned to Kevin and solemnly asked what he was supposed to do with it.

"Club the gophers," Kevin said with the exaggerated patience that a teacher generally reserves for a slow student. "When the gopher pops up, you whop it."

Roth looked at the heads of five molded plastic gophers that were visible in the top of the metal box. "These gophers?"

"Yeah," said Kevin.

"You want me to hit them?"

"Yeah."

"I don't know," said Roth, shaking his head. "Why do you want to club these poor little gophers?"

"Cause it's fun," said Kevin.

Lisa agreed with an exuberant "Ye-e-a-a-h!"

"You want to club these itty-bitty gophers."

The children had caught on to the game he was playing and giggled their affirmation.

"Okay," said Roth dubiously. "Put in the token."

He proved to be a champion gopher clobberer, reacting instantaneously as each head popped up. Rebecca found herself admiring him in an almost clinical way. He really was a spectacular figure of a man. His body was sturdy, broad but not soft, and obviously strong. She admired his ability to control his strength, using the club effectively but without excessive force, and as he laughed along with the children, she found his spontaneity refreshing.

After three rounds of gopher whopping, Rebecca broke through the collective mirth to inform everyone that their number was being flashed on the screen—their pizza was ready.

"All right!" Rebecca called to the two children in the back seat of her car. "You two settle down now. We're almost home, and we have to be very quiet going in the building."

They had taken Rebecca's car because Roth had been driving a pickup truck with only three seat belts in the cab.

The ride had been a riot of silliness and unbridled giggling, and Lisa and Kevin were in a frenzied state. After giving them a stern-aunt look, Rebecca turned her attention to Roth. "The landlady—"

"Doesn't understand the high-spiritedness of children?"

"Doesn't understand *anything* about children and doesn't want to. In all fairness, she really shouldn't have to. No children, no dogs, no more than one cat per unit. It's in the lease." She turned into her assigned parking space, cut the motor, and, after reminding the kids to be quiet, ordered them out of the car and got out herself.

Roth cupped her elbow in his hand as they walked into the complex. "There's something unnatural about outlawing children and allowing cats," he commented.

"Cats are quiet. People who live in this complex like quiet. The ones who want kids and dogs buy houses in the suburbs."

He cast her a questioning sidelong glance. "How about you when you're not niece and nephew sitting? Do you value quiet so much?"

They had reached her door and she fished in her purse for the key. "Yes. Also convenience. My office is less than a mile away, and the Galleria's within walking distance." She stepped aside so that the children and Roth could precede her. "Have a seat and I'll get the chicks."

Kevin's "I will," was quickly followed by Lisa's "Me, too. I'll get them," and they were off.

Shrugging helplessly, Rebecca said, "I'd better supervise. I'd hate to discover they'd conveniently forgotten one of the chicks."

Roth nodded, grinning, and watched her leave the room, noticing and appreciating the feminine sway of her jean-clad hips. She was a little taller than average and sleek, with long legs and arms. Her hair, auburn and highlighted with lighter auburn streaks, barely covered her ears, but it was thick and full and gave the impression of being longer.

With a bachelor's trained eyes, he examined the room for evidence of a male presence. Everything was tasteful, contemporary. The furnishings were not overtly feminine, but he found nothing to suggest that more than one person had contributed to the decor. Apparently she lived alone. *Or she concealed the evidence of her roommate or frequent visitor.* The thought came unbidden and creased his brow into a new frown. He hoped she wasn't seriously involved. He found her attractive, and something about her, a combination of stubborn independence and vulnerability, intrigued him. But then, he'd met her at a particularly vulnerable moment.

She reentered the room carrying a cardboard box and said, "One turkey, eighteen chicks. All present and accounted for." The children trailed apprehensively behind her.

Roth stood up and smiled. "Here. Let me take that."

"Actually," she said, slipping the box onto the coffee table, "this box isn't very heavy. Why don't I carry it while you get the feed? We've only used about five pounds of a forty-pound bag. I'll get it."

"Sure," he said.

She disappeared again and returned carrying a shopping bag from an exclusive store, both hands grasping the handles. She dropped it heavily at Roth's feet. He looked into the bag and back at Rebecca. "It's the best brand on the market, but since when did that store stock chicken feed?"

"That's camouflage," she said. "I don't want to have to explain anything if we run into the landlady. She's upset enough about the kids. I haven't mentioned the chicks."

"Mm-hm," he said in a doctorly fashion.

Rebecca couldn't tell if he was amused or if he disapproved of the subterfuge. But quite frankly, she told herself, she didn't care. Things were difficult enough as it was. "One more piece of camouflage," she said briskly, and went into the small kitchen for a plastic trash bag. "Here kids, hold this open while I put in the box." She turned to Roth. "They should have enough oxygen to last until we get them to your truck, shouldn't they?"

"No problem," he replied, "unless we run into your landlady and have to listen to the story of her life, in which case they'd probably blow the whole caper by cheeping, anyway." His eyes danced with amusement.

Gathering the ends of the bag together, she lifted it gingerly, making sure the box remained upright and didn't swing too precariously. "Here we go," she said to Roth. "Kids, you stay here, I'll be right back."

"This is certainly more exciting than going to a feed store for chicks," he said quietly as they started down the hall.

Rebecca grinned wryly. "I'm glad you're not a man to look a gift chicken in the mouth."

All the precautions proved unnecessary, because they didn't meet the landlady—or anyone else—in the hall. Roth flung the seed into the bed of his truck and put the box on the floorboard of the passenger side of the cab, peeling back enough of the plastic bag to allow plenty of air to reach the chicks. He closed the door and turned to face Rebecca.

After an uncomfortable pause, they spoke at precisely the same moment,

"I—"

"Thank—"

They laughed self-consciously. "Ladies first," said Roth.

Rebecca swallowed and said, "I just wanted to say thank you for dinner. It *was* good to get away for a while." She forced a smile and attempted humor. "You'll have to send me a bill for an apartment call."

"I don't do humans," he said, laughing softly, then he sobered quickly. "I'm sorry about my outburst and all the accusations. I didn't know...I shouldn't have gone off half-cocked..."

She put a hand on his forearm. "It wasn't your fault. I was primed for a good cry." This time her smile was spontaneous and sincere. "It was probably good for me to get it all out."

There was another awkward pause. Each entertained the absurd notion that a kiss would be natural and appropriate, and each discounted the idea as preposterous and inappropriate. Self-consciously Rebecca snatched her hand away from his arm and Roth shifted his weight, clearing his throat.

"Thank you for the chicks," he said stiffly. "Tell the kids I'll take good care of them."

She nodded and forced herself to stop chewing her bottom lip. "Thank you for dinner. The kids were delighted. I haven't been entertaining them much, I'm afraid."

He chucked her chin with a knuckle and smiled. "They didn't seem to be suffering from neglect. You'll be fine. So will they."

She nodded. His reassurance was strangely soothing. Perhaps, she thought, because there was nothing forced or strained in his manner. Somehow that made his comments more valid than the compulsory murmurs of sympathy she'd received from her co-workers at the office.

"Well," he said, "thanks for the chickens."

"And Elvira."

"And Elvira, of course. She'll be the star of the show come Thanksgiving."

His easy smile was contagious. She returned it as she said, "Well, goodbye."

"Goodbye," he said, walking around to the driver's side of his truck.

Rebecca stopped at the entrance to the apartment building to wave and stood there until he'd backed his truck out of the parking space and was headed for the highway.

You'll see him again, she thought.

It hadn't been a permanent type of goodbye.

Chapter Three

Are we almost there, Aunt Becca?"

"Almost," Rebecca replied. "He said about seven miles from the last intersection, and we've gone at least five. Help me look for it. He said it's on the right, and we'll see a sign next to the road and a trailer in the yard next to the house."

About four minutes passed before Lisa announced, "I see it. See it, Aunt Becca?"

Easing her foot off the accelerator, Rebecca said, "Yes, I do. Dr. Lawrence Roth, D.V.M."

"What's D.V.M?" Kevin asked.

"Doctor of veterinary medicine. He's an animal doctor. I told you guys that."

"That's why he knows how to take good care of Elvira," Lisa interjected sagely.

"That's right," Rebecca said as she turned off the engine.

Roth had heard the car and emerged through the door of the screened front porch, waving broadly. It was a country gesture, Rebecca thought, a bit archaic so close to the throbbing Houston metropolis they'd just left.

"Hello," he called.

The children managed only the most cursory of greetings before Lisa got to the heart of the visit. "We want to see Elvira, and Cheeper and Peeper and Tail Feathers."

Laughing, Roth directed them around the house to a shed inside the wire chicken pen. They took off at a gallop, and Rebecca started to follow, but Roth stopped her with a hand on her forearm. "Take your time. They'll find it, and the chicken coop is perfectly safe."

They walked at a leisurely pace beneath the broad branches of a pecan and past a large fig tree. "Pleasant yard," she said.

"I've always thought so," he answered. "I enjoy this place." He stopped in midstep to look at her, his eyes capturing hers, holding them. "You know, I had an ulterior motive for inviting you here. It wasn't just so the kids could visit the chicks or see the pony."

She didn't pretend not to know that their telephone conversation—his casual "I thought the kids might like to see the chicks Sunday afternoon," and her "I'm sure they'd enjoy that"—had been a farce.

He had been inviting her; she had accepted the invitation.

Her silence was answer enough for him—an implied acquiescence. He rested his hand on the small of her back as they resumed walking.

"Do most people call you Becca?"

"Just the kids. Rebecca was a bit tough for Kevin when he was learning to talk, and Lisa calls me Becca because Kevin does."

"Most people call me just plain Roth, but family and close friends call me Larry. Take your pick."

"Roth would be easier around the kids. They'll call you Dr. Roth."

"Okay," he said, wishing she'd picked Larry.

The chicken yard was a tidy rectangle of wood and tautly stretched chicken wire, with the wooden coop positioned at one end. Inside the coop the side walls were lined with roosts and there was a screened hatchery on the back wall. Kevin and Lisa stood on tiptoe, reaching into the hatchery to touch the chicks.

"Look how much they've grown, Aunt Becca," Lisa said.

"My goodness," Rebecca responded, and looked at Roth. "It's remarkable what a difference a few days make if you don't see them every day."

"They'll be big enough for the yard in a couple of weeks. I've still got to build a separate run for Elvira." He lowered his voice. "Did you tell them about the pony?"

"You said it was a surprise."

"You guys want to see what's in the barn?"

Kevin turned to eye Roth curiously. "What is it?"

"I don't want to leave Elvira," Lisa said petulantly.

"You can see Elvira again later. Come on, you can ride piggyback to the barn. What I've got out there has four legs and likes carrots." He knelt and Lisa climbed on his shoulders.

"Is it a rabbit?" she said.

Roth laughed. "Not quite." He paused and helped Kevin lock the door to the coop. "We don't want any wild cats getting the chicks, do we?" he asked, ruffling the boy's hair.

"Nope." Kevin answered importantly.

They paused in the yard while Roth sent the boy into the house for a bag of carrots he'd left on the kitchen counter. Kevin returned almost immediately. "Are you sure it's not a rabbit?" he asked suspiciously.

"I double-dog guarantee it," Roth said.

The barn was old and showed signs of dilapidation, but there was also evidence of recent structural repair. The children spied the pony at the same moment and squealed. "Quiet now," Roth said, squatting so that Lisa could get off his shoulders. "She's young, and she doesn't like loud noises."

"Can we pet her?" Kevin asked.

"You'll have to talk to her first and let her get used to you. Then you can give her a carrot." He demonstrated, approaching the horse slowly, speaking in low, soothing tones, finally stroking her neck with feather-light strokes. "Hello, Ginger. That's a girl. You're not afraid of us, are you?" In the same even tone, he said to Kevin, "Give me a carrot." He gave the carrot to the horse, holding his hand open, showing the children how to avoid getting their fingers bitten.

"Now," he said after the horse had eaten the carrot, "Kevin, you walk over here very slowly and let her take a carrot from you. Good. Good. Now you can pet her neck while she's eating. Now, Rebecca, help Lisa."

"Quiet. Slow. Easy now," Rebecca coached as she and Lisa edged toward the pony.

Lisa was smitten. Her entire face glowed, eyes shining with adoration for the horse. "Ginger," she whispered with awe in her voice, then smiled radiantly as the pony accepted the carrot she offered. The smile became a little-girl giggle, and then it was the adoration on Roth's face that Rebecca noticed. Did he have children? She wondered. Was he a divorcé with children he loved but saw only occasionally? Or had he simply reached that stage in his life when he wanted to have children of his own?

"It's a girl?" Kevin wanted to know.

"That's right. A filly. That's what we call young girl horses."

"How old is she?" asked Lisa.

"About a year old. I just got her this week, and she's missing her mother and the other horses."

"Can we ride her?" Kevin asked.

Roth grinned at the inevitability of the question. "Afraid not, son. She's still too little. She doesn't know how to let you ride her. We have to teach her that next year."

"She's pretty," Lisa said wistfully.

"She certainly is," seconded Rebecca, who knew enough about horses to recognize an excellent bloodline. She looked at Roth, one eyebrow raised. "You didn't tell me your new pony was a quarter horse."

Roth shrugged sheepishly. "She's a beauty, isn't she? I made the breeder promise to sell her to me the moment I saw her."

"Who named her Ginger?" said Kevin.

"That's just a nickname. Her real name is long and silly. The breeder called her Ginger because she's the color of ginger, you know, like you make gingerbread out of."

"Oh," said Kevin, obviously unimpressed. "Why didn't you get a boy horse?"

Roth tweaked the child's nose. "I intend to one of these days, when Ginger's a little older. Then I'll have lots of ponies."

"I love ponies," sighed Lisa.

"How do you feel about kittens?" Roth asked. "I've got a kitten in my office that needs a little love. She had a run-in with a car engine, and I had to do a lot of surgery."

They were given a guided tour of the office from the utilitarian waiting room to the treatment rooms that smelled of antiseptics and alcohol and finally to the small boarding area where animals were left for in-clinic treatment. Muffin was the only current resident and looked pitifully alone in a wire cage. She was snow-white, and her hair was long. It had been shaved in patches for the surgery, and as a result, Muffin looked a bit asymmetrical. She mewed hopefully as they approached.

Roth took her out of the cage, examined her healing incisions with a professional eye, then held her so that the kids could pet her. She purred, closed her blue eyes and tilted her head back to give scratching fingers ready access to her neck. "She likes us," Lisa said.

"Sure she does." Roth frowned. "She gets lonely here."

"Why don't her people take her home? Is she too sick?"

Roth put his arm around Lisa's shoulders. "No, sweetheart, Muffin doesn't have any people. Someone left her on the porch in a box."

"Poor Muffin." Lisa revved up her petting efforts, then cocked her head at Roth. "Why don't you 'dopt her?"

Roth chuckled. "I can't adopt every animal people drop off here. I'll find a nice home for her, though. When her hair grows back, she'll be pretty again, and someone will want her."

"I think she's pretty already," Lisa said.

"So do I, sweetheart. Why don't we take her to the porch for a while? The exercise will do her good."

"Can I carry her?"

"If you're very, very careful," Roth answered. "She's still a little sore." He settled the kitten into Lisa's arms with painstaking care, and they crossed the small parking area near the trailer and the front yard to reach the screened porch.

"There's a plastic ball with a bell in it around here somewhere. Roll it in front of her and she'll chase it," Roth told the kids. "While you're playing with her, Aunt Becca and I are going to set up some horseshoes."

"The set's in the barn," he said as Rebecca fell into step beside him, not really caring where they were going. "Do you think the kids have ever pitched horseshoes?"

"I doubt it," she said, idly musing that she hadn't seen *anyone* pitch horseshoes in years. They didn't talk for a while, but it was a comfortable silence. She felt as though she knew Roth well and had known him for a long time. His patience with the children, his pride in the pony, his gentle treatment of an abandoned kitten-everything confirmed what she had sensed in him when he'd comforted her during her breakdown at the apartment.

Without preamble, his arm reached out to cross her back and his hand came to rest on her waist. Instinctively she moved closer to him, so that their jean-clad thighs brushed lightly as they walked. Almost imperceptibly, his hold on her tightened.

"Why didn't you put the kitten to sleep?" she asked, knowing that would have been standard procedure for a badly hurt stray.

"I don't know," he answered. "At first glance, I thought she was already dead. And then when I discovered she wasn't...she was so tiny and was hurt so bad, yet she was fighting. It didn't seem right not to give her a chance."

They reached the barn. He reclaimed his hand to slide the wooden bar on the door, then stepped back to let her precede him into the cool twilight of the building's interior. Ginger whinnied for attention as they neared her stall, and Rebecca stopped to scratch the pony's muzzle. "You're a sweetheart, you are," she said.

Roth came up behind her and rested his hands lightly on Rebecca's shoulders, then squeezed them gently. He stepped closer to her. "You're a sweetheart yourself," he told her, his voice almost a whisper.

She tilted her head back against his chest and sighed contentedly, and his arms slipped around her to cross just above her breasts. They remained that way for nearly a minute, content with the innocent intimacy of the embrace.

Then, subtly, the nature of the embrace changed. Rebecca's pulse raced as she became aware of his physical response to her, and it took only the slightest nudge of encouragement for her to turn in his arms and loop hers around his waist. "At last," he said, the words rushing from him with frenzied urgency just before his lips brushed over hers, teasing them for an instant before claiming them in earnest.

It was a sweet kiss, not overlong, but it warmed her inside and left her clinging mellowly to him, nuzzling her cheek into the cradle of his shoulder.

Roth stroked her hair and said, "I was beginning to think we'd never be alone."

She cocked her head back and grinned at him. "Dr. Roth, are you telling me you were thinking lustful thoughts all the time you were being so patient with the kids?"

His arms tightened around her suddenly, locking her in a bear hug. "Every second."

She looked up at him, a tantalizing smile of invitation on her lips. "And one kiss is all you're going to do about it?"

"Not by a long shot," he said, and crushed his lips to hers.

She found herself responding to him on two levels at once—physically, to his hard, lean body and hands that caressed as his lips seduced; emotionally, to the sensitive nature and keen intellect that had already earned her respect and affection. The heady blend of sensation and emotion whirled her up into a dizzying vortex of complex sensations. Intense emotions and physical responses melded into a singular yearning, the intensity of which caught her off guard. The nearness of Roth was overpowering—he was solid, warm, wonderful to touch, smelling of musky soap and cologne. Everything else drifted away into insignificance.

He lifted his lips from hers and buried his face in her hair with a sigh. "Oh, lady, you're worth waiting for."

She burrowed her cheek against his chest, listening to the steady pounding of his heart, and thought idly that if he let her go, her knees would buckle. Her own heart was racing, her breathing quickened by the effect this man had on her. She closed her eyes and surrendered to the sweetness of the moment.

Roth parted from her gently, by degrees, loosening his embrace, lifting his chin from her head, retreating at almost imperceptible intervals. Slowly Rebecca's heart resumed its normal rhythm, her breathing slowed, and her legs grew steady enough to support her once again. Roth smiled at her. "We'd better get the horseshoes."

He carried the metal stakes and a large mallet while she brought along the half dozen horseshoes that he had taken from pegs on the back wall of the barn. By the time Roth had driven the first stake into the packed earth a few feet from the driveway, Kevin had wandered over from the porch. "Whatcha doing?"

"Driving stakes," Roth answered. "You and Lisa can toss horseshoes at them. Aunt Becky and I will show you how." He grinned at Rebecca, expecting her to grin back, expecting her eyes to be warm with the new intimacy they had just established. Instead, her features were frozen and her face was pale.

"Don't ever call me that again," she said through clenched teeth.

Roth was dumbfounded. What had he called her? He tried to remember. It was the same thing the kids called her—Becca. Or had he said Becky?

After a moment Rebecca recovered somewhat, but she still appeared shaken. "I don't like anyone to call me Becky."

Roth shrugged helplessly. "Sorry. It was a slip of the tongue. Rebecca. Becca. Becky. What's the difference?"

Rebecca stared wordlessly at Roth for a moment, her face an unreadable mask. What was the difference—he wanted to know what the *difference* was. The *difference* between Becky and Rebecca was only the difference between a shy, gangly adolescent with pigtails and freckles and a self-assured career woman with a stunning figure and highlighted hair; between hands roughened and nails torn by farm chores and hands softened by collagen moisturizers and nails pampered with twice weekly manicures; between a wood frame farmhouse on the outer edge of nowhere and a sleek apartment within walking distance of Houston's Galleria; between luncheon at an exclusive store and a ham sandwich in the kitchen. The *difference* between Becky and Rebecca was the difference between futility and fulfillment, apathy and involvement, misery and happiness, subservience and independence.

Roth's face was the picture of repentance and concern, and his blue eyes were filled with apology for an offence he didn't yet comprehend. "Rebecca?" he said, enunciating her name carefully. "I'm sorry. I didn't know...."

Most people call me Roth. Family and close friends call me Larry. Of course he didn't understand. Lawrence, Larry and Roth were all the same person, all self-assured and easily confident, comfortable and content. She forced a smile. "It's okay. I just... Becky sounds so... crass."

Roth was still flabbergasted by her reaction. He was not a man who quoted Shakespeare, or he might have posed the question in the bard's language: *What's in a name? That which we call a rose by any other name would smell as sweet.*

He didn't pose the question at all. "I won't call you that again," he said flatly, and raised the mallet to drive in the second stake. Having gotten it in place, he stretched an arm across Kevin's shoulders. "Let's go get your sister."

The children caught on to horseshoes quickly and with much more enthusiasm than Rebecca would have predicted. She and Roth left them taking turns and retreated to the porch to sit on the old-fashioned glider. Muffin crept to Rebecca's feet and butted her ankles with her nose, mewing softly.

"Poor lopsided baby," Rebecca said. She lifted the kitten into her lap and scratched her behind the ears. Muffin yawned and her head nodded as she gradually lapsed into sleep.

Roth smiled. "Looks like you've got a friend."

"She was just worn out. Lisa probably gave her quite a workout. Speaking of workouts..." She tilted her head in the direction of the children, from which drifted sounds of laughter and the occasional *tink!* of metal clanking against metal. "They've been needing this. I guess I should have taken them to a park or something."

Roth spread his arm over the back of the glider behind Rebecca, tilted back his head and took a deep breath. "It's nice having people around. Sometimes this place gets lonely."

"Have you ever been married?"

He snapped to attention at her directness. "No."

"I thought maybe you had children. You're so good with Lisa and Kevin."

"No. Never married, no kids."

"But you want children."

"Are you considering getting pregnant? If so, I volunteer...."

It was so obviously a joke that Rebecca grinned and said lightly, "For stud services?"

He laughed in earnest, then sobered, and his gaze wandered to the children playing on the lawn. "I've been thinking about children," he said. "I'd like to have some. I've always been too young or too busy with school and establishing a practice to give much thought to putting down roots. But lately, now that I've settled in here and the practice is... Well, I'm not getting any younger. Of course, I have to find the right woman first."

After the inevitable awkward silence, he said, "Tell me about your job. Do you specialize in any particular type of real estate?"

"I deal mainly with residential. Condos, mostly. Lately I've been dabbling in commercial properties, too. It's a competitive field, hard to break into, especially since the residential market is so depressed now, and so many agents are trying to switch over. Are you often approached about selling your land?"

An unfathomable shadow darkened his eyes; then it was gone. "Not lately. I guess I've managed to convince everyone that I'm not interested in selling." He frowned. "They used to make Mrs. Bachman miserable with their pestering."

"Mrs. Bachman?"

"The woman I bought this place from. Actually, I only bought ten acres and the house. She left the back fifty to her children, and they sold it right after she died."

Once again the shadow dulled his eyes, and he added seriously, "It's a shame to parcel out rice land and put veterinary clinics and machine shops and subdivisions on it. There's relatively little area of the world's surface suited to rice farming." He shrugged.

"But no one wants to grow rice anymore. If I hadn't bought these ten acres, they'd be building convenience stores or gas stations or apartments on this corner."

Once again Rebecca wondered where he had gotten the money for ten acres of prime real estate. A parcel that size could be worth up to half a million, and no veterinary practice was that lucrative. But she said nothing: it was none of her business, anyway.

She complimented his screened porch, and they chatted casually about general topics. All the while, Rebecca stroked the sleeping kitten's head. Finally, at the end of a comfortable lull in the conversation, Roth cocked his head and grinned at Rebecca. "Did you say they allow cats in that apartment complex of yours?"

"Oh, no," said Rebecca, laughing softly. "If I wanted a cat, I'd have adopted one through CAP by now. I love cats, but not snags in the upholstery or smelly litter boxes."

"There's declawing, if it's an inside cat," Roth said halfheartedly. "If it's done right, it doesn't bother the cat."

"That leaves the litter boxes," she countered.

"When I solve that one, the world will beat a path to my door. That'd be better than a new mousetrap."

Kevin interrupted at that moment. Pushing his nose against the screen on the door, he said, "Aunt Becca, we're hungry."

"Don't push on the screen," she said. "How can you possibly be hungry?"

"Growing kids," interjected Roth with a chuckle. "I think we can rustle up something in the kitchen. Why don't you go back and play until we call you?"

"Okay," said Kevin.

"Come on," said Roth, tilting his head toward the front door. "I'll give you a minitour, and you can watch while I heat some biscuits."

"I'm a little tied up," said Rebecca, pointing at Muffin.

Roth dismissed the objection. "Just bring her along. As long as she's next to a warm body, she's happy."

The front door opened into a wide entryway, with doors off either side. "This was originally a dog-trot," he said.

Rebecca nodded. She knew "dogtrots" referred to the early Texas homes built in two halves with a wide, open hallway down the middle to trap whatever faint breeze the hot climate had to offer. With the advent of air-conditioning, most dogtrots had been walled in and incorporated into the house. "When was it built?" she asked. "Do you know?"

"Turn of the century, or a little later," he said. "It's been modernized through the years. Electricity, inside plumbing, a little embellishment here, a little adaptation there. The historical society would cringe, I'm afraid."

"But it's lovely," she said, taking in the quiet elegance of the rooms. "Most of the furnishings are original, aren't they?"

"They're not new," he said, "but most of them don't date back to when the house was built. They've been added through the years, just like everything else. Hence—" he extended his arms dramatically as they approached the kitchen "—conventional, convection and microwave ovens, and an ice dispenser on the refrigerator door."

And a dishwasher, she thought wryly, looking around the cheery room. It was what her profession labeled a "country" kitchen, complete with large windows over the sink and adjacent wall, which bordered a space large enough to accommodate a dinette. "Have a seat," Roth said, indicating one of the ladder-back chairs at the small wooden table.

Rebecca did as he instructed, settling Muffin into her lap again. Roth pulled a plastic bag from an old-fashioned bread bin, a knife from a drawer, and a stick of margarine from the refrigerator. "Betty left some wholewheat biscuits," he explained. "Poor woman thinks I would starve to death if she didn't leave something cooked when she cleans once a week. She shows up with a bag of groceries and hands me the bill, and I tack it onto her fee."

"Would you?" she asked. "Starve to death if she didn't cook for you, I mean?"

"Highly doubtful," he said. "But I wouldn't eat as well. I'm no gourmet, but I can keep myself fed."

He sliced the biscuits and added a dollop of margarine, then slid them into his convection oven. "The kids ought to enjoy wild honey," he said.

Rebecca felt odd as she watched him. She'd never been in a country kitchen and *watched* someone else work, she reflected. She had always been the one, or one of several, working. Working and working and working. Cooking, cleaning, canning. Endless work with only a fleeting effect. A meal was made and served, the mess was cleaned up and it was time to think about the next meal. Wash the breakfast dishes before school, start supper as soon as she got home. No automatic dishwasher, no microwave oven, no shortcuts, no breaks in the routine.

Roth was rummaging in the refrigerator again and emerged from behind the door with a pitcher in one hand and a bag of lemons in the other. "I start with frozen and add the real thing," he said. "What's lemonade without lemon slices? There's some fresh mint, too, if you'd like it. It was early this year."

"Sounds luscious," she said.

He filled a glass and went back to the refrigerator for the mint, dropped in a leaf, and put the lemonade in front of her before setting four places at the table. After putting a ceramic honey pot in the center, he walked to the front door to call the kids.

He led them in like a hen with biddies and made them lather their hands at the sink. When they were seated, he served the biscuits and sat down with them to demonstrate how to use the wooden honey dripper. It didn't take the kids long to catch on, although it was difficult for them to serve themselves properly while their bodies vibrated with their giggles.

They were full as quickly as they had grown hungry, and soon darted back outside to resume their horseshoe pitching. "Let me help," Rebecca offered as Roth began clearing things away.

"And disturb Muffin?" he said. "No way." He made short work of rinsing the dishes and stacking them in the dishwasher; then, after he'd swept a damp cloth over the table, he sat opposite her and they sipped their minted lemonade.

"This is delicious," she said. "I haven't had fresh mint in . . . I can't remember how long it's been."

He covered her hand as it clasped the glass. "I want to see you again," he said. "Next weekend?"

She paused, mentally reviewing her schedule. "I have a business dinner Saturday night," she said, then added hesitantly, "If you'd like to go to that . . . ?"

"That sounds fine," he said, smiling warmly at her. "Will I need a tux?"

She laughed. "I think a suit will suffice."

Muffin's meow drew their attention. She was standing in Rebecca's lap, stretching stiffly.

"We'd better get her back to her cage," Roth said, but they wound up letting her play outside while they tossed a round of horseshoes with Lisa and Kevin. When they finally walked back through the office,

Rebecca commented that he had done a good job of adapting the mobile home into a clinic.

"It's only temporary, I hope," he said. "I'd like to build something that fits with the mood of the house a little better. This trailer isn't aesthetically correct next to the house. Visually, the two are like a mixed metaphor. I'd clone the house if I could."

"Master that and you'll put me out of business," she said. "That would top your litter box trick."

Roth clicked the catch on Muffin's cage and turned to Rebecca. He cradled her face in his hands. "I would never put a nice lady like you out of business," he said, and kissed her.

The rest of the afternoon passed in the same casual way. For dinner, Roth built a wood fire in his brick barbecue pit, then everyone roasted wieners and sausages, put them in crusty rolls and ate them with potato chips, deli coleslaw and some of Betty's homemade bread-and-butter pickles. Dessert was roasted marshmallows.

The kids insisted on a final trek to the coop to say goodbye to the chicks and to the barn to pet Ginger Roth kissed Rebecca briefly after the kids were loaded into the car, then opened the car door for her.

"I liked Ginger," Lisa said as soon as they had turned onto the highway. "I liked Muffin, too."

"How about Dr. Roth?" Rebecca asked. "Don't you like him?"

"Yeah."

"Is he your boyfriend?" Kevin asked.

"Well," Rebecca said, taking a deep breath to stall for time, "he's certainly a nice man, and I enjoy being with him. Don't you?"

"Yeah," Kevin said, "but I wouldn't let him kiss me the way you did."

Chapter Four

Y ou look very dashing," Rebecca said after opening the door in response to Roth's knock. He was wearing a black suit with muted pinstripes, a pale salmon shirt and a striped silk tie. Combined with his natural good looks the effect was quiet, unforced elegance.

"Thank you," he said, walking past her into the living room. He took his time admiring her, his blue eyes lazily appraising and approving the way the asymmetrical neckline of her dress came close to baring one shoulder and the way the soft silk fabric settled over her breasts and hips. "You look rather sensational yourself."

She accepted the compliment with a smile and said, "Have a seat. I was just about to change purses." She disappeared into the hallway and returned a minute later with a small black clutch purse. Sitting down in the chair opposite Roth's, she crossed her long legs at the knee and began transferring essential items from the brown leather bag that had been on the lamp table into the evening purse.

"Where are Kevin and Lisa?" Roth asked, letting his eyes linger on her shapely legs.

"They went home yesterday," she answered, smiling smugly, letting him know that she knew he was looking.

Roth grinned right back at her, refusing to be embarrassed at getting caught doing something as perfectly natural as admiring a woman's beauty. "It's quiet without them."

"Mmm-hmm."

"Is that mmm-hmm it's good quiet, or mmm-hmm it's quiet empty?"

Rebecca stopped what she was doing to look at him. "A little of both. It's good to get back to old routines. I don't have to drive them to school or worry about the landlady—"

"But you miss them."

"Yes. It was so...rowdy when they were here that I used to long for some peace and quiet. Now it's almost too quiet sometimes."

"They're not far away. We'll have to take them to the zoo or something one weekend."

"Mmm-hmm," she murmured noncommittally. Something in the tone of his voice betrayed a yearning for children...and it made her apprehensive. She wanted a family someday, but someday was still a nebulous somewhere-in-time in her mind, and there was no room in her plans for a farmhouse on the far outskirts of the suburbs. Which meant there was no room in her life for any serious involvement with Roth. She would have to be careful with him, watchful for signs that he wanted more than a casual relationship, so she could break away from him before everything got complicated.

The clasp on her purse snapped crisply as she closed it. She stood up. "Ready?"

Roth was on his feet and beside her in a single graceful motion. "Not quite." She faced him questioningly, and he grasped her shoulders gently through the fragile silk of her dress.

Their eyes locked, his making a request, hers granting the permission he sought. By silent mutual consent they stepped closer together, and Roth lowered his head to brush her exposed shoulder with his lips. Then, finding her skin soft and tantalizing, he kissed her in earnest, nibbling at the sensitive area, occasionally flicking it with his tongue as he would a sweet treat too delectable to taste in large doses.

Rebecca sighed and leaned into his strength as his arm slid around her waist to anchor her against him. His kiss seared a path from her shoulder, up her neck and across her cheek, leaving taut, tingling nerve endings in its wake before finally reaching her lips.

An iron-willed restraint on his behalf kept the contact gentle until Rebecca thrust her fingers through his hair and cradled his head in her hands; then his reserve vanished as she hungrily accepted his kiss. Several minutes later they parted, weak and breathless, both aware they had started something and left it unfinished.

Roth was the first to speak, and what he said wasn't what Rebecca was expecting to hear. "I'm glad we got that over with." It was accompanied by a devastating smile.

"Was that a duty kiss?" she asked. "You make it sound as though it were an unpleasant chore. Like cleaning out the gutters."

"I'd hardly put it in the same class as cleaning gutters," he said, laughing. "But if I hadn't kissed you here, I might have lost control entirely and jumped your bones in the middle of the ballroom later. You could incite a man to . . . spectacle-making behavior in that dress."

As they walked to the parking lot, Rebecca was acutely aware of his hand on the small of her back. The prospect of having her bones jumped by Dr. Lawrence Roth was more thrilling than fearsome, though she was certain she'd prefer a more private setting than a crowded hotel ballroom.

The harsh, geometric lines of the Galleria complex were softened by twilight as they approached the massive shopping center, and the colorful displays in exterior store windows took on a glittering, festive air. Roth's truck was but one in a line of vehicles six-lanes wide on Westheimer Road, a major thorough-fare that stretched for miles, seemingly without beginning or end.

"Hard to believe this was bald prairie twenty-five years ago," Roth said while they waited at a red light.

"This was one of the first places I visited when I moved to Houston. It's difficult for me to imagine its not being here." She directed him to the most convenient route into the covered parking area, and they entered the mall on the lowest level. Cool air drifted off the skating rink, a refreshing change from the muggy humidity of the garage.

The rink and the mall were crowded. Teenagers were everywhere—hair carefully coiffed into punk-ish styles and expensive cotton shirts layered to the appropriate degree of motliness—flirting and giggling and communing in the language of the young. Tourists in designer clothes brushed past, chattering in foreign tongues. The atmosphere was charged with chic and reeked of affluence. Both naturally attractive and well dressed, Rebecca and Roth made a striking couple. They looked the epitome of young urban professionals—"yuppies"—but the likeness was only superficial.

Roth, who had been gradually extricating himself from the trappings of city life, would have found the glib label distasteful. The suit he was wearing was the only one he owned and had been purchased hurriedly at one of those discount stores that cuts the labels out of designer suits. He'd bought it and the dress shirt and the coordinated tie to wear to his sister's wedding the previous summer. To Roth, comfort and utility were more important than this season's fashions. He dressed well but sensibly. Jeans and knit shirts were the standards of his wardrobe, worn with western boots in the winter and sports shoes in the summer.

Rebecca, however, would have considered being termed a yuppie a compliment, a realization of goals.

"Young urban professional" was exactly the image she was trying to project. Her dress originally had been priced at three hundred dollars, and, although she had found it on a clearance rack for less than a third of that, that clearance rack had been in one of the leading stores. The hand-me-downs she had been forced to wear throughout most of her childhood had developed in her a yearning and appreciation for quality. Her income was limited, but she was a champion shopper. She knew the Galleria the way many women know the corner supermarket.

For six years, Rebecca had been converting old liabilities into assets. The long limbs and slender build that had made her gangly as an adolescent now contributed to an aristrocratic bearing. The red hair that had inspired the despised nickname "Carrot Top" was hennaed into a stunning auburn and highlighted for an ultra-fashionable look. Shyness had been moderated into a cool reserve that served her

well in real estate dealings. She would have admitted
without hesitation or defensiveness that she was a
yuppie; it was as far away from being a farm girl as
she could get in six years.

They walked past myriad specialty shops selling
everything from athletic shoes to mustache combs
and specialty restaurants that served everything from
crepes to fast food before reaching the entrance to the
hotel, where they took an elevator to the proper level.

A welcome desk had been set up outside the ballroom, and an agent from Land West, the city's larg-
est independent agency, was presiding over a box of
name tags. Rebecca and the agent had become ac-
quainted through a multiple-listing sale Rebecca had
made, and, after the standard greetings were exchanged, the woman shuffled through the file of
tags. "Bruner, Rebecca. Land-Com Realty. Here it
is. And you?" she asked, looking at Roth.

"This is my guest, Dr. Lawrence Roth," Rebecca
said.

The woman looked as though she had just smelled
something unpleasant. "H-how do you do," she
asked curtly, then asked, rather incredulously, "Is
that Roth, R-o-t-h?"

Rebecca could have sworn she detected a note of
hostility in the woman's voice, but Roth gave no in-
dication of having heard it. He accepted the name tag
she made and enlisted Rebecca's help in positioning
it on his lapel. Finally, as they walked into the ball-

room, Rebecca decided she had just imagined an aversion in the woman's attitude toward Roth.

"We'd better find my bosses," she said apologetically.

"Lead, the way, m'dear." His hand rested on her waist as they pressed through the crowd. Rebecca smiled automatically at several agents she recognized from M.L.S. deals or had met at previous industry events. After several minutes of searching for Nita and Carter Vandell, she told Roth, "It was cruel of me to impose an evening like this on you."

"It's a trial I can live with," he said, his mouth tantalizingly close to her ear. She allowed her shoulder to brush into his for a moment and was absorbed in the pleasant warmth of being near him when a voice called her name.

She turned to find her friend and fellow agent, Phyllis, approaching. She made the introductions and watched Phyl's predictable reaction to Roth's good looks and easy smile. Phyl was older and had just celebrated her twentieth wedding anniversary, but she was still frankly appreciative of male beauty.

"Have you seen Carter and Nita?" Rebecca asked.

"They were being buttonholed by Ray Mc-Masters at the door as I came in. Shall we go pay our respects?"

"I suppose we have to," Rebecca answered resignedly.

"McMasters owns Land West, Land-Com's arch competitor," she explained to Roth as they fell into step beside Phyl. "He and the Vandells always manage to feel each other out at these events."

Progress was slow through the milling crowd, but Rebecca discovered that the inevitable bump and shove was not unpleasant when one was being bumped and shoved into a body like Roth's.

The Vandells were still cloistered near the door with their ace competitor. Carter Vandell nodded as the group reached them and introduced his two agents to Ray McMasters. In turn, Rebecca said, "This is my guest, Dr. Lawrence Roth."

McMasters was ostentatiously curt as Roth extended his hand. "Are you the Roth who settled on the Bachman place?" he asked gruffly with all the pomposity of an inquisition judge.

A frown swept across Roth's features, replacing the laconic smile that Rebecca had come to associate with him. "One and the same," he said.

McMasters cocked an eyebrow at him and harrumphed significantly, as though he'd been offered a slice of tainted meat to shake instead of a hand. Carter Vandell looked askance at Rebecca, who shrugged almost imperceptibly to indicate she didn't know what had precipitated McMasters's rudeness. Nita Vandell, sensing an explosive situation brewing, suggested tactfully, "Rebecca, why don't you and your guest go find the Land-Com table? It's supposed to be near the podium. We'll be along directly. Phyl can walk with you."

"What the hell is going on?" Phyl whispered as they headed toward the double doors that led to the rows of white-clothed tables.

"Beats me," Rebecca answered, knowing her face was red with humiliation. "I feel as though I've been sent to the principal's office." She turned to Roth. "What was the deal between you and McMasters?"

Roth shook his head. "Never met the man. Never even heard of him."

Rebecca was still stinging from her employer's rebuke. "I got the distinct impression that he'd heard of you," she snapped.

"My reputation must precede me," he answered wryly.

Suddenly the press of the crowd was irritating, the enforced contact with Roth no longer cozy. Rebecca's career was the means to the life she was creating for herself. Nothing—and no one—compromised her work or her status at Land-Com. It was intolerable. She did not stop to ask herself whether blaming Roth was rational or just; she simply blamed him for her embarrassment.

The welcome had been extended, the invocation read, the meal served. Nita excused herself to visit the ladies' room before the speeches and awards presentation got under way; Rebecca signaled for Phyl's attention and asked, through a tilt of the head and a lift of her eyebrow, if Phyl wanted to go, too. Phyl nodded, and they rose in unison.

"Maybe we can get Nita to tell us what's going on," Rebecca said as they threaded their way between the tables. "The climate has been positively frigid at my end."

"What in the world anyone could have against that gorgeous hunk you dragged in is beyond me," Phyl said.

"So you got the impression it's linked to Roth, too? Carter's been uptight ever since McMasters snubbed him. It's downright weird. Roth insists he's never heard of McMasters."

"There's probably a logical explanation. You know how hyper Carter gets at these functions. And Nita's not about to cross him in front of witnesses."

Frowning, Rebecca said, "Let's hope we can pump some information out of her while she's out from under his thumb."

Nita was primping at the mirror when Rebecca and Phyl entered. She smiled in greeting. "Dinner was better than the usual banquet fare, wasn't it?" They agreed. Then, as if she anticipated the awkward question Rebecca was about to ask, Nita fidgeted nervously and said, "They'll be introducing the speaker soon."

But Rebecca wasn't about to let her get away. "I think we have a few minutes," she said evenly. "The back tables were just getting their dessert when Phyl and I left. I was wondering if I might ask you..." She paused for effect. "I've noticed a bit of tension at the table, and it centers around my guest. Is there something I should know, Nita?''

Plainly uncomfortable, Nita licked her lips before answering. "You're of age and single, Rebecca. Who you . . . see . . . on your own time is your business and no one else's. This Dr. Roth is certainly charming, but you could have used a bit of discretion about bringing him to a business dinner.''

"I don't understand what you find objectionable about him, Nita. There's something you know that I don't, and I wish you'd let me in on it.''

Nita screwed up her face in misery, then gave a sigh of resignation. "McMasters told us all about your Dr. Roth. Land West had a client who wanted to build a subdivision, and they tried for months to buy that farm he lives on. McMasters himself contacted the old woman who owned it, and he was sure she was on the verge of listing with Land West.''

Nita had pulled a cigarette from a leather holder in her purse, and she tapped it against her purse, then lit it and took a deep drag before continuing. "When this Roth fellow appeared on the scene, the old woman balked, and the entire deal fell through for Land West. A few months later they heard she'd sold her place to Roth—cheap. Too cheap.'' She paused long enough to let the facts sink in, then went on. "He gigoloed that old woman out of her land, Rebecca. Watch out for him. He's charming—as a snake.''

"That's just gossip," Rebecca said defensively. "There could have been a dozen reasons the woman changed her mind. McMasters must have jumped to conclusions. Roth is not the kind of man who'd—"

"The old woman's children seemed to think he was," Nita continued imperturbably, not at all repentant about twisting the knife after the way Rebecca had so bluntly pressed her for information. "There was a lawsuit."

"A lawsuit?" Rebecca repeated hollowly, feeling the solid floor turn to shifting sand.

Nita nodded. "Claiming that he had taken unfair advantage of their mother and that she hadn't behaved rationally when she'd sold him the land."

Despising her need to put the question, Rebecca nevertheless asked, "What was the outcome?"

Nita blew out a generous cloud of smoke and shrugged. "The American justice system's gone to hell in a bushel basket. There's no law against gigoloing, and no defense against foolishness. She was foolish, not crazy, so there was nothing the judge could do about the doctor keeping the land."

This information about Roth settled deep inside Rebecca like a heavy lump of stone. He was a charmer, all right—down-home friendly with boy-next-door good looks. And he seemed so sincere. The perfect con man and gigolo. A flush crept up her neck and over her face when she realized how easily she'd been taken in. And the worst part was that she had brought him with her to a public function where his presence would cause embarrassment not only for her but for her employers and Land-Com as well.

Nita took advantage of the lull to make her escape, leaving Rebecca and Phyl staring at each other. "Do you believe it about him?" Phyl said.

"If there was a lawsuit, there must be something to it."

Phyl arched her eyebrows skeptically. "He didn't strike me as the gigolo type. Such lovely blue eyes, and that wonderful smile."

"Maybe the reports of the death of Mr. Goodbar have not been exaggerated," Rebecca said humorlessly.

Somehow she managed to sit through the after-dinner speech and the awards presentation, when what she wanted to do was run away from Roth and the Vandells, from the entire situation.

"Would you like to stop somewhere for a drink?" Roth asked as they left the ballroom.

Rebecca skillfully extricated herself from contact with him as he attempted to put his hand on the small of her back. "It's almost eleven," she said. "I have to work tomorrow."

"I was hoping we could talk," he said, and he meant it. They'd begun the evening splendidly, as friends, and now they were strangers. No doubt about it: she was giving him the cold shoulder, one far different from the soft, enticing shoulder he'd kissed earlier. It had metamorphosed from sweet ambrosia into solid marble, hard and cold, and all because that puffed-up jerk from Land West had snubbed him. That damned lawsuit was still hanging around his neck like an albatross. She must have heard something about it—some twisted gossip spawned of half-truths and innuendo. It was the only thing that could explain her change of attitude. He'd have to talk to her about it, make her understand.

But not in the truck while he was concentrating on traffic, he thought. He wanted to sit down with her and give the matter his full attention. The drive to her apartment was short but gravely silent.

"Well, good night," she said at her door. The finality in her tone carried an additional message: Goodbye and good riddance.

He raised a hand to stop the door closing. "I'm coming in."

Her expression became a mixture of incredulity and skepticism. It held no humor or tolerance, and certainly no invitation. "It's late."

"If I believed that was the real reason you weren't inviting me in, I'd respect your wishes. But you know as well as I do the sudden chill treatment I'm getting has nothing to do with what time it is."

"Please leave."

"Do you want to discuss it out here in the hallway, or in your apartment where we can have some privacy?"

"We have nothing to discuss."

"What did you hear?"

"I'll call security. We have a cop who lives in the building."

"Fine. I'll have a seat and wait for him."

So, Rebecca thought in exasperation, the real Lawrence Roth reveals himself—stubborn, self-centered and arrogant. She sighed resignedly and stepped aside, then followed him to the middle of the room. They sat where they'd sat earlier, he on the sofa, she on the chair facing it.

For a full minute they glared at one another in a tense, silent standoff. Finally, Roth said bluntly, "What did you hear?"

"That you got a very sweet deal on the land you own."

"And that makes me an untouchable?"

"Do you care what I think? I heard you like your women a little older and a lot richer than the likes of me."

A muscle twitched in Roth's jaw. "There's a name for what you're calling me. Why don't you just spit it out."

"Forgive me. I was trying to be polite. I've never called anyone a gigolo before. But then, this is the first time I've been duped by one."

Too furious to sit still, Roth rose and pretended to study an abstract painting on her wall. Finally he turned to face her. "You actually believe that about me?"

Believing it was difficult. In his suit he looked so...legitimate. Suave. A man of integrity. *Exactly the way a con man and a gigolo wants to look,* Rebecca reminded herself. "You wooed that old woman out of her property," she accused bitterly.

His voice was ugly, edged with sarcasm. "Yes, Rebecca. Veterinary medicine is just a sideline with me. My real avocation is being a gigolo. Just look at what I've gotten out of you. For the price of a pizza and a few sausages, I've wangled eighteen chickens, a Bourbon Red turkey and a dinner in town. Not a bad exchange. Nothing to brag about to my fellow gigolos, but I'd say I worked a profit, especially if I throw in that kiss earlier this evening. That ought to be worth something on the open market. I could have sworn you cared a little bit about me from the way you poured yourself into it."

Reflexively, she bounded to her feet and raised her hand to slap him, but controlled herself in time, and let it fall limply to her side. "I'm going to call the cop if you don't leave."

His smile was ugly. "No self-respecting gigolo lets himself get hauled off to jail. So long, sweetheart. It's been nice bilking you. I'll think about you when I'm gathering eggs." It was a succinct exit speech, yet he remained frozen in place.

"Just go!" Rebecca said through clenched teeth. "I meant it about calling the cop. He's just four doors away."

Roth stalked to the door and jerked it open savagely, but paused again when he was halfway through it. The sarcasm had faded from his voice. "I

liked you, Rebecca. I respected you. I didn't have
you pegged as a person who would convict someone
on gossip and innuendo without even hearing his
defense." His voice became a whisper hoarse with
disgust. "You're no more capable of independent
thought than one of those chickens you gave me. If
you ever need your gutters cleaned out again, give me
a call."

Rebecca stared at the door after he'd slammed it,
paralyzed by the venom in his words. She felt a
strong need to bawl like a baby, but instead emitted
a guttural cry of frustration, remembering the last
time she'd felt this emotionally pent-up, the day he'd
come for the chicks and she'd broken down and
sobbed on his shoulder. He'd been so gentle with her,
so kind and understanding. How could she possibly
reconcile that man with the arrogant brute who'd
just left, a gigolo who'd cheat an old woman out of
her land?

Easy, she thought bitterly. *A convincing act of
gentleness and understanding is the stock-in-trade of
a gigolo.* She'd been taken in by his act, just like the
old woman.

She took a shower and scrubbed herself rather
savagely with a soapy washcloth, then stood under
the spray and then let the hot water cascade over her
body while she shampooed her hair and waited for
the instant conditioner to do its work.

The words of the old show tune she was humming
came to her suddenly. *I'm going to wash that man*

right out of my hair.... Was that what she was doing? Washing him out of her hair and scrubbing him, symbolically, out of her life?

No, she thought later as she tried to sleep. It was what she had been *trying* to do. He was irrevocably out of her life but remained stubbornly in her mind. She kept hearing his words: *I didn't have you pegged as the type of person who'd convict someone on gossip and innuendo....*

She'd never had herself pegged that way, either. The first doubts about her snap judgment and ready acceptance of gossip as gospel began niggling away at her conscience.

Chapter Five

Rebecca hesitated a moment before cutting the engine. There were still several cars in the small lot, and she was not sure she should be barging into Roth's clinic unannounced. In fact, she wasn't even sure why she had come in the first place. She'd been out to see a parcel of land in the area and had passed his clinic. Then, on the way back to town, she'd turned into the drive. No forethought, no soul-searching, no conscious decision making. She'd simply put on her blinker and turned.

She hesitated a few minutes before getting out of the car. It was not too late to back out. All she'd have to do was drive away, and he'd never know she'd been there. But finally, ignoring her reservations, she stepped out of the car, squared her shoulders, and walked to the office door.

Everyone in the small waiting room looked up as she entered, and she felt a fresh wave of panic and doubt. She was considering leaving when the woman behind the reception counter greeted her cheerfully. Rebecca forced a smile in return and stepped up to the counter. "I'd like to speak to Dr. Roth when it's convenient."

The woman, identified as Kathy Parks by a plastic name badge, asked Rebecca's name; then, after running her finger down the column of an appointment book, she asked, "Did you have an appointment, Ms. Bruner?"

"No, I was hoping . . . I just wanted to talk to Dr. Roth for a moment."

"Is this concerning a pet?"

"No." She felt conspicuous and foolish. "I . . . I just wanted to speak with him a moment."

"I'll tell him you're here. You understand that we have to take our appointments first?"

"Of course," Rebecca said. She sat down next to an elderly gentleman with a poodle perched in his lap. On the other side of a corner table, a girl about eleven years old was trying to calm a Garfieldesque tabby that lent credibility to the old adage, "Nervous as a cat."

Rebecca shuffled through the stack of magazines on the table. *Cat Fancy, Dog Fancy, Horse and Horseman* and *Reader's Digest*. She picked up the

Reader's Digest and thumbed through it just to have something to do with her hands.

Her restlessness must have been apparent to the man with the poodle, because he looked at her and asked, "You have a pet?"

Rebecca shook her head. "I live in an apartment."

"Never could understand how people could stand to live on top of each other that way, like boxes shoved next to each other, with no yard and no animals," he said.

"Some people are too busy for yards and animals," Rebecca replied with an indulgent smile.

"Always had some kind of animal on the place," the old man reminisced. "Used to keep hounds for hunting. Always had a cat around to keep mice away. Now all I got left is Bubbles here. Nearly split my sides laughing when Ellie—my late wife—brought her home." He laughed again at the old memory. "Didn't look like no dog I ever seen; looked more like a curly-haired rat and wasn't worth a plug nickel. Still isn't, but I didn't have the heart to get rid of her when Ellie passed on. She doted on this dog like a kid, talked to it like a baby." He stared into space, seeing the past, as he scratched the poodle's ears. His eyes misted. "Closest thing I got to having Ellie with me."

"She must be a lot of company for you," Rebecca said, marveling at the tenderness in the old man's gnarled, leathery hands as he stroked the dog.

"Mr. Lewis," called the receptionist, "bring Bubbles on back." The old man rose and carried the dog toward the treatment rooms, petting her and jabbering to her as he walked. Rebecca tried to get interested in the *Reader's Digest* but was distracted when a new arrival—a basset hound leading its owner into the clinic by its leash—spied the little girl's cat and leapt toward it barking and snarling. The child squealed as her cat ground its claws in her skin and arched its back, hissing.

The basset hound's owner defused the crisis by tugging sharply on the dog's leash and ordering it to sit down where it could not see, or be seen, by the cat. Rebecca went back to the *Digest's* account of the ongoing battle against a disease that was currently in the news.

The minutes she waited seemed to drag interminably. A dalmatian emerged from the treatment area with his master and glowered at the cat and the basset hound while his owner paid the fee at the counter; a few minutes later, the receptionist directed the girl with the cat toward the clinic area. Rebecca shifted in her seat, crossed and uncrossed her legs, and had given up on the magazine by the time a teenage boy came in carrying a ferret. The receptionist returned, checked the young man's name on the appointment pad, then walked through the room to flip the Open sign on the door to Closed.

She stopped in front of Rebecca. "I'm sorry it's taking so long. It's been a busy day."

Rebecca smiled. "You warned me." The woman was almost back at the counter when Rebecca asked, "Excuse me, but is Muffin still in the back? I'd enjoy holding her, if it's all right."

Kathy considered the unexpected request. "I'll see if it's okay. I don't know why it wouldn't be," she said, and disappeared into the back of the building. Half a minute later she was back. "Dr. Roth is getting Muffin for you."

There was not even enough time for a protest before Roth, wearing a lab coat over jeans, entered from the treatment room area with Muffin cradled in one arm. A broad smile lightened his entire face when he spied Rebecca, and he walked toward her in long strides, reaching her before she had a chance to stand up.

Bending over, he surprised Rebecca by kissing her on the cheek before gently depositing the kitten into her lap. "Your friend's been missing you."

Rebecca looked full into his face and their eyes locked in a significant exchange. He wasn't talking about the kitten and they both knew it. To the others in the waiting room, his hand coming to rest on her shoulder must have seemed an innocent gesture. To Rebecca, the contact felt intimate, but she made no effort to escape. Instead, she found her own hand rising to cover his as though it were moving there of its own volition. Roth's eyes narrowed and he removed his hand from under hers with painstaking gentleness. "I'll be finished soon," he said, and left.

Rebecca turned her attention to the kitten in her lap. The hair around her incisions had grown, and Muffin was not nearly so lopsided as before. In fact, Rebecca had to concede that the kitten with the tragic past was maturing into a handsome cat.

Time dragged by. The old man came out with Bubbles, the woman with the basset hound was summoned to the treatment area, the little girl with the cat left, the boy with the ferret was escorted to the treatment area.

Long minutes later, Rebecca heard hound's toenails clicking across the vinyl tile as the dog was led outside, and finally, the teenager with the ferret made his way to the door, followed closely by Kathy, who paused long enough to say, "Larry said to tell you he'll be right out. I'd stay and chat, but my babysitter gets upset if I don't pick up my daughter by six."

Restless, Rebecca rose and wandered into the hallway behind the reception counter. The sound of movement drew her to the open door of a room at the far end of the hallway. Roth was inside, wiping a stainless steel tabletop with disinfectant. He looked up and smiled self-consciously when he discovered her standing in the doorway. She was unprepared for the effect his smile had on her.

"Just finishing up," he said, swiping one last time across the glistening steel. After stashing the spray bottle of disinfectant in a cabinet under the table and tossing the brown paper towels into a plastic-lined garbage pail, he said, "Come on."

She followed him into the room that housed the cages for hospitalized patients. There was a bar of soap-on-a-rope hanging by the sink there, and he lathered his hands with it. The woodsy scent she had come to associate with him wafted through the room. "Smelling like disinfectant is an occupational hazard, but I don't have to tolerate it after hours," he said. He rinsed his hands thoroughly, slid off his lab coat and deposited it in a canvas laundry bin. "Now I shouldn't smell like puppy dogs and kitty cats, either."

"Or ferrets?"

"Slippery little devils. Did you ever try to give one an injection?"

"Not recently."

"Lucky you," he said, and frowned slightly. "I wish people would leave wild animals in the wild. But if they're responsible enough to want to keep their pets healthy and vaccinated, I can't turn them away." Cocking his head inquiringly, he asked, "Did you change your mind about wanting Muffin?"

Rebecca felt her cheeks burning. "No...I... You were right. I'm not the sort of person who usually judges people based on gossip and innuendo."

A few steps brought him close enough to embrace her. "I'm glad I was right." His movements swift and smooth, he bent his head to kiss her as his arms slid around her waist, but she flinched away from him. He raised his hands as though contact with her burned him.

Rebecca attempted to swallow the lump that had formed in her throat. "Before I make any judgment at all, I want to hear your version of how you got your land."

Roth chewed on his lower lip as he studied her face. Rebecca could almost hear his brain working as he considered her challenge. Finally, he cupped her elbow loosely and said, "Let's get out of here. Do you want to carry Muffin or put her back in her cage?"

"I guess you'd better put her back in the cage."

They went out the back door and across the lawn to the barn, where Ginger whinnied impatiently on hearing their approach. Roth nuzzled the pony's nose with his hand. "Hello, girl. Ready for some exercise and some fresh food?" The filly followed him through the door that led to the small corral, where she broke into a playful trot. Rebecca laughed at the horse's high-spiritedness, so fraught with the universal exuberance of youth. "She's grown."

Roth's pride in Ginger was obvious as he watched the filly cavort in the pen. He grinned and glanced toward Rebecca. "She ought to," he said wryly. "She eats like a horse."

Rebecca stayed in the corral watching the pony while Roth cleaned the stall and put fresh food and water in the troughs. He joined her when he had finished the chores, coming to stand wordlessly by her side. For several minutes they stayed there, close but not touching, aware of each other's presence but not speaking.

"We'll leave her out a while," Roth said. Rebecca nodded and followed him through the barn and across the lawn to the porch. He gestured for her to sit on the glider, and their arms brushed lightly as he settled beside her. For a long moment they both stared awkwardly into space, neither knowing how to begin to bridge the gap between them.

"Mrs. Bachman had an old horse," he began finally, "Nappy, short for Napoleon. He'd outlived his usefulness, but she couldn't bear the thought of getting rid of him. Nappy was ailing, and her regular vet suggested she have him put to sleep. I don't know why she called me—she probably went down the list in the Yellow Pages—but she asked if I'd come out and give her a second opinion, and I drove out after office hours because I enjoy equestrian work and I wasn't getting much of it."

He paused, took a deep breath, exhaled slowly. "After I'd examined the horse, she insisted on making a cup of coffee, so I went with her to the kitchen, and sat at the table while she made it and cut me a slice of chocolate cake. I told her the truth, that Napoleon was dying of old age."

Again, he paused. "She wanted to know if he was suffering and whether I thought she should put him to sleep. I told her he wasn't in any pain. Then she asked if there was anything we could do for him. I told her he would benefit from special feed and periodic vitamin injections, but I made it clear Napoleon wouldn't live over a few months in any case."

He lifted Rebecca's hand from where it lay limply in her lap, threading his fingers through hers, and rested it on his thigh, which was solid and warm under the soft denim of his jeans. She felt very near him, not just physically, but emotionally. He was sharing more with her than words and anecdotes; he was sharing his feelings. She felt his compassion and his affection for Mrs. Bachman, the kindness that was a part of his nature.

"After thinking about it a while," he continued, "she put her hands on her hips and cocked her head at me and said, 'Will you give 'em?' and I . . . well, I couldn't refuse her. She was so . . . lonely, and holding on to an old friend."

He paused to clear his throat. "It became a ritual, the weekly injection for Napoleon, and then the coffee and chat. Eventually coffee included dinner. Nothing fancy, just meat and potatoes and fresh vegetables from her garden. She told me what it had been like when she and her husband were dairying, and about her children and how none of them were interested in farming. After her husband died, they kept trying to get her to sell out and move to a condo, where she wouldn't have to work so hard."

He smiled, remembering. "She was a feisty old woman. She used to sniff with disdain over her kids' attitude, and over the fact that they didn't understand her any better than to think she'd be happy in a condominium. And then there were the real estate vultures . . .''

Rebecca tensed involuntarily at the unpalatable phrase, and he cocked an eyebrow at her. "That was her term, not mine. This parcel of land was a plum, and they were all after it. Mrs. Bachman was old and unsophisticated, but she wasn't naive. She knew they were racing to get her property listed before she died."

"And Ray McMasters and his crew were right on top of her," Rebecca said flatly. "Land West didn't get to be the biggest through lack of aggressiveness."

"I didn't meet any of them," Roth said. "Mrs. Bachman just told me about them. She was . . . dismayed over the changes in the area. Twenty years ago it was all dairies and rice farms. Then they built the first subdivision, and the country club and the shopping centers, and more subdivisions and schools. It all happened so fast that she had a hard time dealing with it. And her kids went off to college and never came back, except as visitors. She was proud of them, but at the same time she felt betrayed that they had rejected her way of life, which urban sprawl was progressively destroying."

Rebecca debated a long time before asking, "How?"

"How did I wind up with the farm?"

"Mmm," she said, relieved that he had phrased the question for her. They were both staring through the screening, watching a large pecan tree sway gently in the slight breeze.

"Quite by accident," he said. "One day she'd had a rough session with a persistent real estate agent, and she was on a tear. After she'd ranted on for a while, she planted her hands on her hips and said, 'I've got a good mind to sell my land to you; you'd appreciate it. I'd *give* it to you before I'd sell it and see them build several hundred ticky-tacky houses on it, so close together you can hear the neighbors snore.'"

He gave the glider a nudge. "I didn't think anything of it. She got on tangents from time to time, and she was riled up after her confrontation with the real estate agent."

"It must have been McMasters."

"I honestly don't know who it was. But the next time I came, she asked if I'd ever thought of buying a house. I told her I'd been too busy getting a practice established to think about it."

He smiled reminiscently. "'You need a good woman to settle you down,' she told me. 'Then you'd think about a home.' It wasn't the first time she'd told me I needed a woman. When she said that, I'd put my arm around her and tell her she was all the woman I needed, and she would laugh and call me a fresh kid."

He tilted his head toward Rebecca. "There was nothing ugly or kinky about it. She was like a grandmother to me, and she liked having a kid around to mother. That's the way she thought of me, as a kid."

From the bottom of her heart, from that part of the mind—or the self—that accepts without proof, Rebecca believed him.

"One day," he continued, "I came out here and she said, 'I've decided to sell my place to you. For what they sell one of them fancy subdivision houses for.' I was astonished. Tongue-tied. I explained to her that I couldn't possibly take care of so much land. I couldn't afford the *taxes* on all her property.

"'Then I'll sell you the house and however much you can take care of,' she said. She was . . . she could be...a very persuasive woman when she put her mind to it. So I bought the house and ten acres for a hundred thousand dollars, with the agreement that I would take possession of it after she died. Her kids were hopping mad, but there was nothing they could do about it while she was alive. They waited until she died, then filed a suit claiming I had imposed undue influence on her. Fifty acres wasn't enough for them; they wanted the ten she'd sold me, too. The case was thrown out of court, but the stigma lives on."

"Kept alive by fools," Rebecca said, her voice harsh with self-incrimination. She turned her head to face Roth. "I'm sor—" she began.

He pressed his fingers over her lips. "It's okay," he said, brushing a light kiss on her cheek. "What matters is that you're here." And then he silenced her protests with another kiss. Afterward, she rested her head on his shoulder, her hand on his chest, and sighed.

"I never believed you were a gigolo," she said softly. "I tried to, I...pretended to, even to myself. Roth, it was my boss who made the allegations, and that confused me. It was weak of me not to stand up to her. And when I confronted you and you didn't deny or explain, I tried to convince myself that I had been duped."

He hugged her closer. "You're here now. That's what counts. I missed you, Rebecca. More than I should have. The fact that you...that *you*...believed the lie hurt more than it should." Lifting her chin with his fingertips, he said, "I care what you think because you're important to me." Her name floated from his tongue like the lyric of a love song, cherished and sweet, just a fraction of a second before he kissed her again.

There was no logic in her response to him, only physical sensation and emotional reaction. He was a man, warm, strong, virile, and he desired her. His body against hers, the rapid beating of his heart, lips that savored as they conquered, left no doubt of it. And she was important to him. He had said so, but his delight at seeing her and his willingness to forgive her lack of faith in him were more revealing than words. Now, the softness of her lips and the trust implicit in her surrender told him that she understood and accepted.

When the kiss ended, she remained in his embrace and nestled her head against his chest, listening to the strong, steady rhythm of his heart while the glider rocked smoothly to and fro. They were comfortable, at ease with one another, content just being close.

Abruptly, the phone rang, a harsh intruder. It seemed an almost anachronistic invasion, effectively breaking the spell of timelessness that enveloped them.

Roth hugged her shoulders before he reluctantly lifted his arm from around her. "I don't know who that could be," he said. "Yesterday I would have been hoping against hope that it was you."

While he dashed inside to answer the phone, Rebecca sat up straight, crossed her legs and wondered if she was getting in over her head. She hadn't planned to be here, hadn't planned to stay once she'd listened to his version of how he'd gotten his land, most definitely hadn't planned to cuddle with him in the porch glider and have him tell her that she was important to him.

Roth was . . . Roth. Wholesome, yet sexy. Sincere. A salt-of-the-earth type of guy, a guy hungry for a woman to settle down with. She'd be a lucky woman, Rebecca speculated. Roth would be a loyal husband and a devoted father.

But Rebecca had plans for her life, and they didn't include a nice guy with a place in the country. She had worked too hard to get where she was headed to let a little chemistry lead her astray. If she moved anytime soon, it would be into a high-rise condo with a view on the outskirts of downtown, not a farmhouse in the suburbs. She had her eye on a building that was going up along lower Westheimer. Maybe someday she'd want children, but her biological clock still had some time to run, and she wasn't ready yet for anything as mundane as child rearing.

Now that he was out of sight, she could think straight, and her straightest thought was that she had to cool things before either of them got further involved than they already were in what had to be an impossible relationship. Her mind was made up by the time she heard him returning to the porch. She would tell him she was glad that they'd gotten things cleared up between them, say goodbye and leave. With dispatch, before his wholesome charm and woodsy after-shave fogged her senses.

He leaned against the door, muscular arms akimbo, after he had closed it behind him. His expression was pleasant but serious. "I've got to go out to a horse ranch in Katy. They've got a mare foaling. Why don't you come with me?"

It was time, Rebecca thought. Time to say, "So long. Nice knowing you. See you around." Time to leave, she was sure of it.

She smiled up at him and said, "Okay."

Chapter Six

I'll see if I can find some clothes for you. You wouldn't want to wear that suit into a barn.''

"I wore it into yours," she said dryly.

"You were just passing through. We might be a while, and you might want to... sit down or something."

She followed him into the house and stood in the hallway while he rummaged through the closet in his bedroom.

"You wouldn't consider wearing a T-shirt that says, 'Veterinarians do it with care,' would you?"

"Not on your life." Poking her head through the door, she added, "It really isn't imperative that I change clothes. Shouldn't you be hurrying?"

"Bingo," he said, pulling out a pair of cotton beach pants. "Now for a shirt. Even if we hurry, the mare will have dropped the colt by the time we get there. The trainer is attending her. I'll just give momma and baby the official once-over, as a matter of procedure. The owner's out of town. Here, this ought to suffice," he said, producing a tropical-print shirt. "I've got to run out to the clinic to pack my bag. You remember where the bathroom is, don't you?"

The pants were a bit big, but there was a drawstring in the elasticized waistband, and the legs were wide enough to roll into loose cuffs to just below the knee. Roth, back from the clinic, greeted her with approval as she returned to the living room. "You do things for those clothes I never could."

"The buttons are on the wrong side of the shirt."

"But the curves are in all the right places." He put his hands under her arms and slid them lingeringly down her sides, his thumbs brushing the sides of her breasts before he reached the indentation of her waist, paused, then traveled down to rest on the gentle swell of her hips. "All the right places," he repeated, with a look in his eyes that made her feel weak all over.

Then, with a sigh, he kissed her on the forehead and said lightly, "We'd better get going."

It took close to half an hour to reach the ranch, and they chatted amiably along the way. "Do you really have a T-shirt that says, 'Vets do it with care?'" she asked.

"I haven't worn it since vet school. It was a gift. One of those white elephants one gets stuck with."

"From someone who knew the truth of what was written?" she teased.

"From someone who was anxious to find out if it was true."

"Did she?" Rebecca regretted the words as soon as they were out of her mouth. What had possessed her to ask him such a thing?

Roth said flatly, "She found out about one vet student." After a strained silence, he added, "That was a long time ago, Rebecca. There's no one else in my life now."

"I was only... I wasn't—" she stammered.

"Weren't you?" He rested his hand lightly on her thigh, forcing her attention to him. "I wouldn't romance one woman when I'm sleeping with another. I like women, but I haven't the time, energy or inclination to juggle them around. That's schoolboy stuff."

"What was the name of that ranch you told me to look out for?" Rebecca asked, delighted to have found an escape from a conversation that was making her edgy.

"The Rocking Bar."

"Well, turn around. You just passed it."

Roth made a U-turn and drove through the gate and up the long driveway. "Past the main house, left at the fork, large red buildings. I think we just found the stables," he said, braking the truck in front of a long wooden building painted a deep red.

"Some barn," Rebecca said. "Do the horses dress for dinner?"

A middle-aged man wearing faded jeans, worn boots and a gray baseball shirt met them at the door. "You Dr. Roth?" he asked, extending his hand. "I'm Jackson, the Cliburnes' trainer. Thanks for coming on such short notice."

Roth introduced Rebecca, then asked, "Do we have a foal yet?"

"One here, another on the way. You're gonna get a bonus on this one. Goody Four Shoes dropped a filly, and Classy Chassis just went into labor."

"Two at once?" Roth asked. "That's rare this late in the year."

"They came into season the same week and were serviced by the same stallion," Jackson said with a chortle of laughter. "That stallion didn't know how he got so lucky."

"Any problems with the first mare?" Roth said in a professional tone.

"Nope. Went smooth as silk."

"And the filly?"

Rebecca, who had walked slightly ahead of the men as they became immersed in stable talk, settled the question of the filly with a gasp of delight as she reached the stall housing the new foal and its mother. "She's beautiful, Roth. Look at those eyes."

Roth gave the filly a careful look, then turned to Jackson. "No emergency here. What about the other mare? Any signs of distress?"

Jackson nodded toward the last stall in the long row. "See for yourself. I wouldn't have left her long enough to lead you in if she'd been in any trouble. She's close."

The mare was stamping restlessly in the stall, breathing heavily. Jackson automatically reached up to pet the horse's muzzle while Roth, speaking softly to the mare, palpated her swollen middle. "Everything seems to be progressing normally," he told Jackson. "Do you want me to intervene in any way?"

"Don't see why," Jackson said. "Horses been foaling since before they thought of veterinary schools."

Rebecca watched as Roth grinned at the stable manager and nodded in agreement. Men, she thought, certainly had peculiar rituals of communication.

"I didn't know the Rocking Bar was raising Arabians these days," Roth said.

"It's Missy Cliburne's doing," Jackson explained. "She talked her daddy into buying the mares. She's partial to Classy Chassis, here."

Suddenly Classy Chassis whinnied loudly and lay down in the clean hay. Roth, standing behind Rebecca slid his hands around her waist as they witnessed the ancient miracle of the renewal of life.

"A colt!" Jackson announced as the newborn foal made its first attempt to steady himself on impossibly spindly legs. "The Cliburnes are going to be sorry they missed all the excitement. 'Specially Missy. Wait'll I tell 'em about little Windborne Charlie here."

"You've named him already?" Rebecca said.

"Oh, yes, ma'am. The Cliburnes had names picked out for the foals either way. Goody's filly will be named Matilda the Hon. I 'spect we'll call her Tilly for short."

"Matilda the Hon?" Rebecca asked skeptically.

"Don't laugh," Roth whispered in her ear. "Horse people are sensitive about their names. It's not easy coming up with original ones for the registration."

She leaned into his solid strength as they watched the colt's ill-coordinated test of his legs. "He's a handsome colt," Rebecca said.

"Good stock," Roth replied. "Momma's a fine-looking horse."

"His sire was a champion," Jackson interjected, reminding them that they weren't alone—and Roth that he had work to do.

Reluctantly he withdrew his arms from Rebecca and directed his attention to Goody Four Shoes and her filly, talking in a soothing voice as he examined first the mother, then the foal. "All's well in this stall," he told the trainer, who had grown fidgety watching someone else take care of the horses that were normally his private responsibility. "If you'll calm the mare, I'll get the filly inoculated."

Skillfully he led the still wobbly-legged baby out of the stall, talking to her in a low, soothing monotone. "Here, Rebecca, keep her still while I get the hypodermic ready."

"I get to touch her?" she asked, delighted by the prospect. "I've been dying to give her a hug, but I was afraid to ask."

Roth tweaked her nose with his forefinger and grinned. "Silly, why didn't you say something?"

"I didn't think the mare would allow it." Roth's grin grew into a full-fledged laugh as he opened his bag and withdrew a syringe and several rubber-topped plastic medicine bottles.

Rebecca was on her knees hugging the filly, giggling as the little horse nudged her shoulders in search of what only its mother could provide. "Hold her steady," Roth instructed, and proceeded to inject the antibiotic solution beneath the foal's skin.

Increasing the rate at which she was stroking the filly's neck, Rebecca made a face and offered sympathy over Matilda the Hon's fate at the hands of "that mean old man sticking you."

Roth frowned at her. "Some respect, please, nurse. Don't bad-mouth the doctor in front of the patient."

"Volunteer help doesn't have to follow protocol," she said. Roth harrumphed at her impertinence and guided the filly back into the stall with her mother. "Meanie!" Rebecca said with an exaggerated sniff of disdain. "Just rip her from my bosom when we were getting to know each other."

"As appealing as your bosom is to certain ones of us, it's momma's bosom this filly is interested in," Roth countered. Little Matilda the Hon illustrated his point by immediately probing for the mare's teat and suckling hungrily upon finding it.

Roth moved on to Classy Chassis's stall and repeated the examination procedure. Windborne Charlie was still damp as Rebecca knelt to hold him. "He's pure sweetness," she told Roth over the colt's head. "So sweet." The foal startled her by nudging his nose against her cheek, and she laughed softly and stroked his tiny muzzle. "Hang in there, Charlie. Dr. Roth's almost finished and you can go back to momma."

After returning the colt to its stall, Roth shook hands with Jackson and congratulated him on the two healthy foals, then praised the excellent condition of the stables. The trainer swelled with pride and blushed unexpectedly when Rebecca shook his hand and thanked him for allowing her to visit.

Roth picked up his bag and put his free arm across her shoulders. When she made no move to leave, he hugged her and prompted, "Ready?"

"I hate to leave them," she said, looking from colt to filly. "Are foals always so sweet?" she asked as they started back to the clinic.

"Sweet? Yes. Not all of them are as handsome as the ones we just saw, but they're all sweet. This was the best kind of call, caring for healthy, fine animals. It's not so pleasant when an expensive stallion gets a bellyache. There are times when I wish I could start a treatment session by administering a tranquilizer to owners and trainers."

He cocked his head toward her curiously. "You act as though all this were new to you. Didn't you have horses on the farm where you grew up?"

"Horse," she corrected. "Always one. The first horse I remember died of old age when I was eight or nine, and Daddy kept the one he got after that until it died, a year or so after I left. The Bruner barn was nowhere near as fancy as the stables we just left."

"Few barns are."

"We had a sow once. I used to play with the piglets in the spring." A smile of nostalgia touched her face, then faded, and she added softly, "They grew up so fast."

Roth heard the echo of loneliness in her voice and tried to imagine her as a child, giggling and having fun with playmates that would soon become too big to be managed. He wanted to ask about her childhood, about the painful memories of her early life, but he decided to ask another time. She was excited over the foals, and he didn't want to break that happy mood. He reached for her hand and held it in his on the seat between them.

He squeezed her hand. Rebecca turned her head toward him and smiled. Silhouetted by the fading sunlight that was filtering through the side window of the truck, his profile took on a classic perfection as he directed his attention back to the highway. His curly brown hair capped his head like the marble waves on the bust of a Roman emperor.

She felt uncommonly serene in Roth's company. The feeling had begun when he'd welcomed her to the clinic, then had grown when he'd silenced her apologies and justification with a kiss. He'd forgiven her lack of trust without making it seem like some grandiose gesture of absolution.

And she could not get the scene in the barn out of her mind, the birth of the colt. A celebrated birth, to be sure, but what they had witnessed was more than the arrival of a perfect creature engineered by selective breeding. The thrill of the moment had derived from an acknowledgment of the colt's perfection, not as a member of a rare breed, but as a living creature.

To observe his innocence, his wobbling attempts to stand, his triumph at getting to his feet, had been to observe the universal challenges and struggles of a new life. She had been awed by the drama, and she had sensed, as he'd held her in those few moments, that Roth had been awed, too, despite the fact that he had surely witnessed similar scenes countless times before.

That he could feel this wonder each time somehow made him special to her. Such sensitivity was rare; it drew her to him like a physical force. She felt that she and Roth had shared something unique and magical; felt close to him and yearned to be even closer. The intensity of what she was feeling both scared and thrilled her at the same time.

She wondered why she had agreed to go with him on the call just seconds after having resolved to say goodbye and never see him again, but she was glad she had gone. Such ambivalence was rare for her. For years she had been forging ahead in dogged pursuit of very definite goals, never wavering or questioning what she wanted, never regretting the things she'd had to give up, and *never* allowing an obstacle to stand in her way.

Roth did not fit in with her master plan to make it to a high rise with a view. If he'd wanted that out of life, he'd have had it by now; instead, he had a farmhouse that was half a century old and five miles outside the city limits. And that made him an obstacle. He was the first obstacle she'd ever regretted having to overcome—the first, in fact, to which she'd even given a second thought.

The yellow light on his porch broadcast a welcome through the darkness of early evening as they approached the house. Roth helped her from the cab of the truck, put his arm across her back and his hand on her waist. "How about taking potluck in the kitchen? I think there's some cold roast beef, and I could toss a salad."

"No," she said. Realizing they were halfway to the house, she stopped in midstep and looked up into his face. "I'm not going in, Roth."

"Not... But I thought—"

"I came to build a bridge and I built it," she said. Unable to face the pain in his eyes, she looked down at herself in his clothes and tried to laugh. "I'll have to send your clothes. I'm afraid Charlie got them a bit dirty." He was about to protest again, but she said quickly, "Walk me to my car?"

Setting his face into a mask of stoicism, he turned with her still under his arm and they walked toward the clinic parking lot. Halfway there, he said, "Are you going to tell me why you're leaving, or do I stay awake all night trying to make some rhyme or reason out of it?"

"Because I have to," she said miserably, and then, because she couldn't stand being unfair to him again, she said, "I can't stay. I...I'm in a vulnerable frame of mind right now." They had stopped walking, and she lifted her hand to cradle his cheek, pleading for understanding with her eyes. "I'm afraid I'm a little too awed by everything tonight to be logical right now."

He hardened his hold on her waist, drawing her to him. "Maybe it's not the time for logic between us."

"But it has to be," she said, too quickly.

Roth was puzzled by the panic in her voice. "Is there someone else?"

"No."

"Some*thing*, then. Tell me what it is, since I have to live with it. I can usually take a brush-off, but this one doesn't make any sense."

"I'm beginning to care about you, and I can't let that happen."

He would have been exasperated with her if she hadn't looked so abjectly miserable. "For God's sake, why not, Rebecca?"

She stiffened and took a breath to fortify herself. "Because I've never met a man so ready to meet the right woman, and I'm not the right woman for you, Roth."

He drew his arms from around her and crossed them over his chest. "And how did you arrive at that profound conclusion?"

"Because you live here. It's where you belong, in this rambling farmhouse, surrounded by all this land." She thrust her shoulders back and raised her chin, defying the tears that threatened her composure. "It's not what I want, Roth. It's what I've left behind, not where I'm headed."

"And where are you headed, pray tell?"

"To the tallest building I can afford to live in, with a panoramic view of downtown."

Roth chewed on that piece of information a moment, then ran his forefinger over her cheek. "Are you sure that's where you belong?"

"I'm sure as hell going to find out."

"You won't like it, Rebecca. You're too warm a woman to be happy in a cold, lonely tower."

She smiled bitterly. "My tower's going to have central heat and a fireplace."

"Then I hope you get your ivory tower. And I hope it makes you happy."

She wasn't expecting him to kiss her, and certainly not with such devastating gentleness. Nothing but that gentleness could have set her senses reeling so and left her filled with such doubt. She was limp when he drew away from her, and no longer sure that leaving him was the right thing to do. In fact, it seemed a preposterous thing to do. If he had asked her into his house at that moment and led her to the bed with the iron headboard she'd seen in his bedroom, she would have gone with him.

But Roth didn't ask. He brushed an errant curl from her forehead and said, "When you're sitting in front of that fireplace, think of me. Remember tonight and our visit to the Rocking Bar Ranch. It was special, wasn't it?"

Like their parting, her smile was bittersweet. "Yes," she agreed. "It was special."

Chapter Seven

As she passed Roth's clinic, Rebecca forced her eyes to the highway ahead and concentrated on what Aubrey Weston was saying about the area through which they were driving. If she hadn't had a client with her, she would have driven seven miles out of the way to avoid passing the clinic because she knew she'd be tempted to stop and see him.

"With all this growth in the face of a depressed housing situation, I'm sure the area would support the type of project I have in mind. I liked the looks of this piece of property when I was out yesterday," he was saying.

"I checked the charts," she said, careful to keep the discussion crisply professional, "and the parcel we're going to see is over a mile from the nearest floodplain. You'd be high and dry, Mr. Weston."

"You're very efficient, Ms. Bruner," he said, his tone softening. "Why don't you call me Aubrey, and I'll call you—"

"Rebecca."

"Rebecca. If I decide on this piece of property, we'll be working together on it, so we might as well be on friendly terms."

As long as you don't confuse friendly with intimate, she thought, but said coolly, "All right, Aubrey." He was a big man, too beefy, too rawly masculine for her taste, and there was something predatory about his attitude in spite of the aloof, all-business demeanor. She hadn't been the least surprised when he told her he was in the physical fitness industry, and she wouldn't be surprised if he told her that he was a retired professional athlete.

"You say it's four acres?" he asked.

"Three point nine. We can walk the boundaries, if you like. There's a fence along the back and one side. And roads on the other side and in front, of course. It's a high-visibility corner tract."

Weston shifted position and stretched his arm over the back of the seat behind Rebecca's head, trying to make it seem like an attempt to get comfortable in the small confines of the car. Rebecca suppressed a grin at his technique, glad they were less than a mile from the property so he wouldn't have enough time to push it too far.

The shell driveway was quite long. She parked about fifty feet from the house and they got out of the car. "This is roughly the center point of the parcel," she told Weston, then leaned against the fender of the car while he looked the land over with a critical eye.

"Those trees on the periphery are good," he said. "We could leave most of them, maybe put in an outdoor jogging trail."

Rebecca nodded noncommittally. She liked to give prospective buyers room to discover a piece of property on their own. At his request, they walked to the rear boundary, a substantial five-foot fence that had been put in by the developer who owned the land beyond; then they followed it to the side fence, which was a dilapidated post-and-barbed wire job in need of repair. Rather than walk it all the way to the highway that bordered the front of the property, Weston turned abruptly and cut across to the car.

"The house is about forty years old," Rebecca said. "Two bedrooms, one bath, country kitchen, formal dining. It's a converted dogtrot design, charming, like so many of the homes from that era." *Like Roth's.* The thought came unbidden.

Weston shrugged. "The house doesn't really matter." Then he added, smiling, "But we might as well have a look, for curiosity's sake."

Rebecca was not afraid, but she didn't relish the idea of going through the house with Weston. "I wouldn't want to waste your time," she said. "If you're not interested . . ."

"I insist," he said with a note of sacrificial gallantry. "You seem enchanted with it. Let's have a look."

"Notice the waves. The glass in that window must be original," she pointed out as she worked with the lock. Weston, predictably, was as unimpressed by the old glass as Rebecca was by his heavily spiced cologne. He was standing unnecessarily close for such a hot afternoon.

The house was stuffy and warm, and she left the door open to catch the breeze. Weston took off his sports jacket and hung it over his shoulder on two fingers. He followed her through the living and dining rooms with a marked lack of interest, and was similarly uninterested in the wooden cabinets in the kitchen.

"Are the bedrooms this way?" he asked, gesturing toward the wide hallway.

"Yes. One forward, one back, with the bath in between."

"Show me."

With a keen awareness of what was about to transpire and powerless to forestall it, she crossed the hall into the rear bedroom. He stepped uncomfortably close behind her and said, "You're a very beautiful woman, Rebecca, and you're not wearing a wedding ring."

Her body tensed involuntarily, and she swallowed before turning to look him squarely in the eye. "I'm not selling anything but real estate, Mr. Weston," she said.

"The commission on this property would be quite substantial."

"I wouldn't want anything to influence your decision to buy the land or not to buy it except the land itself."

"And after the decision's made and the deal is closed?" he challenged.

"We shake hands."

A frown slowly formed on Weston's handsome face. "You're hard on a man's ego."

"We've established that I'm in real estate, not public relations."

"Let's get out of here. It's hot."

It wasn't much cooler outside, but Rebecca heaved a silent sigh of relief to be out in the fresh air. Weston took his time looking over the property again while she leaned against the fender of her car. Despite the come-on, Rebecca sensed that he was seriously interested in the parcel.

On the way back to town, he outlined what he would do with the land if he bought it, describing a family fitness center with gyms and weight rooms, and an indoor pool and handball courts.

"And the house?" she asked.

"It'd have to be torn down."

"Oh," she said, then felt extremely dense. Of course the house would have to be torn down. That's why he'd been so unconcerned about it. "That's a shame."

He shrugged. "I guess so. But that's the way things are. Not much you could do with an old house like that, anyway."

Rebecca made a noncommittal sound and remembered Roth's saying he wished he could clone his house and use the clone for a clinic.

"I've got to think about it a few days, but I liked the property," Weston volunteered. "The location's ideal, and those trees in the back are a plus." It was the last either of them said until they reached Rebecca's office and he shook her hand. "Thanks for showing me the property, Rebecca. I, uh, can call you Rebecca again, can't I?"

"Certainly, Aubrey."

"I'll be back in touch in a few days, one way or the other."

"I'll be expecting your call."

He had not let go of her hand. "After this real estate business is settled, I plan to get on with the business of pleasure, Rebecca. Thought you might like fair warning. I'm going to be in full pursuit."

Just what I need, she thought, and wondered why this nice-looking, obviously successful man didn't do a thing to her pulse rate, while a country horse doctor had the power to make it race.

Weston called two days later with a bid on the property. It was several thousand under the asking price, but she was not surprised when the sellers jumped at the offer. The parcel had been part of an estate, and the heirs were anxious to liquidate—the heirs of an elderly man who'd played with children and grandchildren and great-grandchildren in that lovely old home that was going to be torn down and hauled away in pieces. Rebecca couldn't get the house—so like Roth's—out of her mind as she attended to the paperwork that was involved in completing the sale of the property.

The actual closing took hours longer than anticipated. By the time the money had been exchanged and the papers signed, it was close to noon, and Weston launched his promised campaign of seduction by inviting Rebecca to lunch to celebrate the transaction.

Somewhere between the soup and the salad, between the detailed description of the fitness center Weston was building and a discussion of the heat wave that was plaguing South Texas, Rebecca found herself talking about the house that was to be torn down. Without even acknowledging to herself what she was doing, she asked, "If someone wanted that house and was willing to move it, would you sell it?"

"If a woman like you wanted it, I'd give it away. It'd save me the trouble and expense of tearing it down and hauling it away."

"I was serious, Aubrey. Are you?"

"So the question wasn't just rhetorical. Do you have a little piece of property somewhere you want to put it on?"

"No," she said, shaking her head. "I don't. I just know someone who might like it."

"A client?"

"A friend."

"Then it's yours. Provided it's moved by July first."

"Hey, not so quick," she said, laughing softly. "I'll have to show it to...my friend."

He picked up on the hesitation like finely tuned radar. "What does *he* plan to do with it?"

Rebecca dropped the forkful of salad that was halfway between her plate and her mouth, and narrowed her eyes. "How did you know?"

"Body language," he quipped. "Bodies are my business." Rebecca put the sidetracked salad into her mouth and chewed. Very slowly. And Weston asked, "Is it serious?"

"No," she answered, not intending to lie, but not entirely sure she was telling the truth, even to herself. "He's just a friend. A veterinarian. He might like to convert the house into a clinic."

"Well, if he's interested, just make sure he moves it before we're ready to break ground. You'll take care of the paperwork, won't you?"

"Aubrey?" She was dumbfounded. "You're really going to *give* it away?"

"I wouldn't feel right asking for money for it. I was just going to pay someone to tear it down."

"That's cockeyed logic."

"Your beauty befuddles my brain. You wouldn't consider coming to work for me teaching aerobic dancing, would you? We'd train you, of course."

Laughing, Rebecca said, "No, thank you. I think I'll stick with real estate."

"I was afraid of that. Too bad. You've got a great body. You'd be a knockout in a leotard."

Weston paid for their meals at the register near the door, and they walked out into the foyer of the restaurant. After he'd replaced his wallet, he fished in his side pocket for the keys to the house. "You'll need these. When you show your friend."

"I don't know what to say," she said.

"You could start by telling your friend he's a very lucky man."

"To be getting a free house? I think he'll figure that out for himself."

"I wasn't referring to the house."

"But..." The denial died on her lips, and an awkward silence yawned between them.

He pressed the keys into her hand, closing her fingers around them with his. "You have my address in Atlanta. Mail me the papers and I'll sign them. When I get moved to town, maybe we'll run into each other when you're not so hung up on that veterinarian of yours."

"He's not *mine*," she said, flushing profusely.

Weston cocked an eyebrow. "Then I'll be sure to get in touch when I get back to town."

It was Tuesday when Weston gave Rebecca the keys to the old house. She fretted all week over whether or not she should approach Roth about it, and if so, how. Nothing in the etiquette books covered giving someone a house just a few weeks after walking out on what might have been a meaningful relationship.

She thought up a lot of excuses not to show it to him. She knew nothing of his financial situation. She might be putting him in an embarrassing position if he couldn't pay to have the house moved. Or he might not like the house. Or he might just feel awkward about the entire situation. She herself had felt a bit peculiar about it when Weston had said he'd *give* her the old building.

One by one she discarded the excuses. If he didn't want the house, couldn't afford to move it or didn't feel right about taking it, he could always refuse. She wasn't wheeling it up to his front door; she was simply showing it to him and letting him know it was available.

Late Saturday afternoon, she drove to his house, halfway hoping he wouldn't be home, or that he would tell her he was busy, or that he would be entertaining a statuesque blonde on the sofa in his living room—anything to get her out of the ridiculous situation she'd managed to get herself into. He was going to think she was schizophrenic at the very least when she came driving up to his house after her last, dramatic exit scene. When he heard what she'd come for, he'd probably call the men in white coats.

And if he was entertaining a statuesque blonde on the living-room sofa, she'd strangle him—and the blonde—and plead insanity.

Chapter Eight

Roth tapped firmly against the bottom edge of the board with his hammer while applying pressure on the outer edge with his left hand. Sweat beaded his forehead as he strained in the summer heat. When at last it was wedged into position, he reached into the utility pocket of his carpenter's apron for a nail.

The crunching of tires on the shell driveway attracted his attention and he looked up, shielding his eyes against the afternoon sun with his hand, hoping it was not an emergency that would take him away from the job he'd started. He recognized the gray sedan immediately and felt his pulse quicken. What the hell was she doing here? Hadn't she made her position perfectly clear the last time he'd seen her? Resuming his work, he drove the first nail into place with savage force.

The car squealed slightly as it drew to a halt in front of the house. She needed a brake job or, at least, to have her brakes checked; he'd have to mention it to her.

He watched her as she stepped from the car, his eyes hungrily taking in every detail of her appearance, particularly her smart yellow slacks and crisp white camp shirt. She was as alluring as ever, he thought. When she was almost within comfortable conversation range, he fished in his apron for another nail, positioned it, and hammered away.

Rebecca stopped about ten feet from him and watched him work. When he finally looked up, she could feel the tension crackling in the air between them. Forcing a smile, she said, "Hello."

Roth nodded, without speaking, then dug in the apron for another nail, hoping his hands appeared steadier than they felt. She had set the rules. He'd be damned if he'd let her know the effect she had on him.

Rebecca swallowed the lump that had formed in her throat. Under the short utility apron, he was wearing shorts that fitted snugly over his muscular thighs and a sleeveless beach shirt that clung to his chest in the summer heat. He was blatantly male. Wishing her mouth weren't so dry, she said lamely, "Making some repairs?"

He shrugged. "You have to stay ahead of these wood houses."

"Mmm," she agreed. She felt like screaming, hitting him, anything to tear away the blanket of tension that shrouded them, but she forced herself to stand stock-still until he picked up the conversation.

"What brings you here?" he asked finally.

Her tongue was tied in knots. "I... There's something I want you to...something I want to show you." The way he stood there enjoying her discomfort was unforgivable. "I thought...if you weren't busy...but you obviously are, so..."

Retreat was all she could think of. She turned and walked at a brisk pace toward her car. He ran after her, grabbed her by the arm, spun her around. In the summer heat, the short sprint had winded them, and they were breathing heavily as they stared at each other. The air sizzled between them. "Don't go," he said, devouring her with his eyes. "I want to see whatever it is you came to show me."

"I... It's not here," she said. "We'd have to drive..."

"Okay. Just give me a few minutes to get cleaned up. There's no hurry, is there?" She shook her head. He put his hand on her shoulder and slid it down to her elbow. "Come on in. Have some lemonade while you wait."

She had intertwined her fingers and was staring at her hands to avoid facing him. She nodded and he cupped his hand over her elbow and guided her toward the house.

She sat at the kitchen table and watched while he halved a lemon and ground each half over the fluted knob of an old-fashioned juicer. He had begun the lemonade making by dissolving sugar in hot tap water, and now he added cool water and the lemon juice and stirred. He filled a glass with ice, dropped in a leaf of fresh mint and poured the lemonade. "Voila," he said, putting it on the table in front of her. "I'll join you as soon as I can make myself presentable." He leaned to kiss her on the forehead. "You smell good," he said, grinning, then left the room.

I ought to, she thought, recalling the small fortune she'd paid for the perfume she was wearing. It was a scent she reserved for special occasions—like giving away houses.

"Do I get to know where we're going?" he asked later as they buckled their seatbelts. He'd showered and shaved, and the woodsy scent of his after-shave permeated the interior of the car.

"Now you smell good," she said evasively, and started the engine.

Roth shifted on the unfamiliar seat and feigned indifference. "I guess you aren't going to tell me until we get there."

Rebecca chuckled wryly and said, "Curious type, aren't you?"

Roth responded by shifting restlessly again and uttering an inarticulate noise that might have been categorized as a grunt.

"If you must know," she teased, "we're going to see a clone."

"Oh, goody," he said dryly, "I love science fiction adventures."

Rebecca switched the car radio to a soft-rock station, and neither of them said anything more during the ten-minute drive to Weston's property.

The empty house appeared neglected and forlorn at the end of the long driveway. Rebecca drove as close to it as she could and parked the car. "Well?"

"Well, what?"

"What do you think?"

Impatience invaded his voice. He was not a man who liked guessing games. "It's a house."

"You really should be a detective," she said glibly. Pulling the keys from her purse, she jangled them in the air. "Let's have a look."

Standing in the wide hallway, Roth noted the living and dining rooms to the left, the bedrooms to the right, and the kitchen beyond the dining room with a growing sense of deja vu. "It's a lot like my house."

"It was built around the same time," she said, raising a living-room window in the hope of drawing a breeze. She let him wander, discovering subtle differences. He disappeared through the door from the kitchen to the rear of the hallway and reappeared a minute later.

"You told me once you wished you could clone your house for a clinic," she said. "Would this be close enough?"

A fist closed around Roth's heart. She was just trying to make a deal, earn a commission to put toward that pie-in-the-sky dream of hers. He'd hoped in the face of reason that . . . well, he was a fool. She was just drawing on their friendship to make a buck. "Are you selling it?" he asked, his voice bitter. "Giving me first crack before it goes on the market?" He thought if she offered him a discount on her commission, he might wallop her.

"I've already sold it. I sold it almost a month ago. They're going to build a health spa on this land. The house was...is...expendable. They're going to tear it down unless . . ."

"Unless?"

"Unless you have it moved before they break ground for the spa. It's yours, Roth, if you want it."

"Mine?" he said, blinking in incomprehension. "I thought you said you weren't selling . . ."

"Not selling, Roth. Giving. It was given to me; I'm giving it to you, if you want it. There'd be some minor fees involved with transferring the title, and I don't know how much it costs to have a house moved. But if you want it and you can move it . . ."

Roth looked as though someone had physically knocked the breath out of him. "Let me get this straight. You sold this house to someone who was going to tear it down, and he gave it to you and you're giving it to me?''

"If you want it and can get it out of the way before the construction crews get here."

The incredulity mirrored in his face struck her as funny, and she burst into laughter. He looked at her a moment as though she'd lost her mind, then laughed, too.

"You don't have to decide immediately," she said after they had sobered. "You could bring out an electrician and plumber..."

"Are you insinuating I would look a gift house in the plumbing?" he teased, then, more seriously, added, "I'll check it out, but I'd be a fool not to take it, even if it needs some work. It's exactly what I've visualized but never believed possible." His eyes met hers significantly. "You knew that, didn't you?"

"I... It just fell into my lap. It wasn't like..."

"You know me so well, Rebecca." She hadn't realized he'd moved, but suddenly he was holding her, and she was putting her arms around him and raising her face so he could kiss her. Nothing else mattered at that moment, not the stuffy heat in the old house, not their differing goals, not her resolve to remain uninvolved with him.

The kiss was like a feast after a fast. They were hungry for each other, for the feel of body against solid body and the taste of lips on lips. Rebecca felt herself flowing into him, melding against him, reveling in his strength, rejoicing in the virility that could make her unadulteratedly female.

When he jerked away from her abruptly and turned his back to her with a violent, miserable, "Damn," it was like a physical blow. He spun to face her again, but only after there was distance between them, a few feet to protect him from the powerful urge to touch her. "Nothing's changed, has it, Rebecca? You've given me something, a dream that seemed impossible, but that's the only reason you're here, isn't it? And now that you've given it to me, you're going to leave again, just like before."

Turning his back to her, he stared unseeing through the window for a few seconds, then slammed his fist against the wooden window frame. "Damn it, Rebecca, I was just getting over you."

The need to comfort him was overwhelming. He was so miserable that not to do so would have been less than human. She touched his shoulder with her fingertips, carefully, cautiously, then heard his ragged sigh and felt his tense muscles relax as his shoulders drooped in defeat. His face, as he turned toward her, was the picture of vulnerability.

"I couldn't forget you," he said softly. "That *would* be the impossible dream. But I had managed to stop thinking of what might have been and accept what really was. And then you drove up this afternoon, and it was as though you'd never left. I was afraid to talk to you, afraid you were an apparition, that I'd willed you there, and if I spoke to you, you'd evaporate."

A muscle twitched in his tightly clamped jaw, but his eyes never left her face, as though he were memorizing it so he could conjure it up again in the future. His fingertips brushed her cheek as lightly as dandelion fluff floating on the breeze. "Now I'll have to start forgetting you all over again."

Rebecca's throat ached. She wanted to cry but couldn't allow herself to. Uttering his name in more a gasp than a whisper she flung her arms around him and buried her face in his shoulder. "I never meant to hurt you."

The fierceness with which she clutched him surprised him. He rocked her gently, patting her back, the wounded soothing the wounded. His fingers combed through her hair, pushing it away from her face. "You couldn't help my falling in love with you. Even I couldn't have prevented that. It was as inevitable as the sun rising in the east."

"I'm not the right woman for you, Roth," she said, knowing it sounded empty and inadequate.

"I love you. That makes you the right woman."

She pulled away from him, walked to the window. "We want different things. Sooner or later we'd hurt each other."

Stepping behind her, he wrapped her arms around her and across her shoulders. "Why is that high rise so important to you, Rebecca? What would you have there that you couldn't have with me?"

"A view," she said breathlessly. "A view alive with people going places and making things happen." She rested her head against his chest and relaxed as he hugged her still closer to him. Wrapped in his arms, she sensed his need to listen and understand. "I used to look out the kitchen window when I was doing dishes and see nothing but land and animals. Land and animals."

She paused and fortified herself with a deep breath. "The first time I saw Houston's skyline, it was the most beautiful sight I'd ever seen—the crisp, straight lines of the skyscrapers, the feeling in the air of things happening, the idea of so many people inside those buildings making important decisions...just the sheer excitement of it all. I vowed then that someday I'd become a part of it, that I'd have a window where I could look out and feed on that excitement anytime I wanted to."

"Were you that lonely growing up?"

"Yes," she said somberly. "Lonely. And bored. Mother died when I was seven, and Helen and I took over the housework, so there wasn't much time for anything but school and work. Then Helen won a scholarship and left home, and there was twice as much work, and no one to talk to."

Trying to picture her in his mind as a lonely adolescent, Roth pressed a comforting kiss on her temple. "Your father?"

"My father was a simple man with simple beliefs."

She sighed, and an edge of bitterness sharpened her voice as she continued. "Simple, but totally inflexible. As long as there was food on the table and a roof over our heads he was happy. He couldn't understand why we wanted more than that. He didn't understand why Helen and I wanted to go to college. In his mind, we didn't need to. He thought we should be content to stay at the farm taking care of him until some farm boy decided to do us the honor of marrying us so we could go take care of him instead."

After a pause, Roth said softly, "They called you Becky?"

She nodded. "I hated the sound of it because I hated myself. I was a gangly kid with long, scrawny legs, afraid of her own shadow. Helen had been married about a year when I came to Houston. After I'd been here a while under her influence, I began to feel like a different person from the girl from Deadwood."

She paused. "One day Helen marched me to the beauty shop to have my hair professionally styled and my nails manicured, and I didn't recognize the girl in the mirror when they'd finished. I just knew her name wasn't plain old Becky. She was a Rebecca, at least."

Gently coaxing his arms apart, she stepped out of his embrace and turned to face him. "Just as I know that she'd never settle for less than what she wants."

A sickening realization numbed Roth. Now that he understood her compulsive need to be part of the bustling big-city life, he comprehended what a formidable foe the city was. And he was unsure how to fight it. Another man would be one thing, but a city—how did one fight a city?

The silence stretched interminably between them. Finally Rebecca said, "I'm sure you want to look through the house more carefully. I'll wait on the porch."

A sense of relief swept over her as she stepped outside, and, feeling weak-kneed, she sat down at the top of the concrete steps that led to the porch and listened to the sound of footfalls on old wood as Roth moved around inside the house. Dredging up the past, stirring up old feelings and remembering old insecurities had drained her. She had confided things to Roth that she'd shared only with Helen and Greg, things she'd kept carefully hidden behind a cool, confident facade.

For the first time since she'd realized who she was and what she wanted, Rebecca felt threatened, threatened by the alternative Roth offered her. It was an attractive alternative, one that could divert her attention from the goals she'd set and make her doubt the wisdom of her judgment.

And doubt was the one thing she could ill afford. Despite the facade, she hadn't come far enough from that timid little farm girl, wasn't confident enough yet to face self-doubt. If she left the path she'd mapped out for herself, she might get lost again, and the prospect was intensely frightening.

Because she was attracted to him, she was vulnerable where Roth was concerned. He had the potential to undermine the goals that were literally the foundation of her identity. For the sake of the person she had formed out of that lump of timidity from Deadwood, she had to stay as far away from him as possible. And, for her own safety, he must never, never know how vulnerable she was where he was concerned.

"I closed the window and locked it." His voice startled her as he stepped onto the porch; she had become so absorbed in her thoughts that she had ceased hearing the sound of his movements in the house, had not heard him approaching.

Standing up, she dusted the seat of her slacks and answered, "Here's the key to the door." The lock made a clicking sound as the tumblers fell into place. He extracted the key and extended the ring to Rebecca, but she shook her head. "Keep them. The house is yours if you want it. If not—" she shrugged "—the keys don't matter."

They didn't converse on the ride home. Rebecca pulled into Roth's driveway and stopped, leaving the engine running. "Let me know when you've made a firm decision about the house," she said in a professional tone. It was clearly a dismissal.

Roth made no move to leave the car. "I've already made a firm decision. I want it."

"I'll start the paperwork, then," she said. "Shall I send the papers directly to you, or will you have an attorney handling your end of the transfer?"

Her brusque, businesslike demeanor nettled him. She was giving him a house, damn it! Didn't that bespeak some form of friendship? Did she have to be so cool and concise? When he spoke, his tone was icy enough to make hers seem warm. "Send them to me directly. I trust you implicitly—personally and professionally."

Apparently unruffled, she nodded and, after a pause, said, "I'm glad you're going to preserve it. I hated the idea of it being torn down."

Biting back a sharp retort about her touching concern for an old country home that had no view, Roth said, "Will you stay for a while?"

He didn't miss the way she suddenly stiffened. "I can't today," she said evenly.

"Can't or won't?"

She blinked, then studied her hands as they rested on the steering wheel. "Please, Roth. I can't stay. We both know why."

No longer able to resist the urge to touch her, he pressed the back of his hand to her cheek. It was soft and cool under his knuckles. "I'd make you stay if I could."

Be quiet, Roth. Please. And don't touch me. I can't think when you touch me. Rebecca felt her breathing grow ragged as she strained for control. If she looked at him, she'd be lost. She stared at her hands on the wheel, concentrating her attention on the diamond-and-ruby ring she was wearing.

Finally he withdrew his hand and said bitterly, "Emily Post never covered a situation like this. Thank you for the house, Rebecca. I hope you'll come see it when I get it all set up." He yanked the door handle and Rebecca heard the door open with its characteristic creak. Involuntarily, she turned her head toward him. Roth sighed raggedly, then leaned across the seat and kissed her gently, briefly, on the cheek. "Goodbye, Rebecca. And have your brakes checked. They're squealing."

"Goodbye, Roth."

She drove away feeling as though something were being physically wrenched from inside her.

Chapter Nine

For the fourth time, Rebecca checked her reflection in the mirror. What are you afraid you'll find? She chided herself. Stray threads? White specks on your shoulder? *A neon sign flashing, "Don't pressure me, Roth. I might succumb because I haven't been able to get you out of my mind," across your forehead?*

The invitation had arrived the preceding week. "You are cordially invited to an open house at the Dogtrot Animal Clinic." The date. The time. The address. A handwritten plea from Roth: "Please come. It won't be complete if you don't."

The clinic was even more charming than she'd anticipated. Freshly painted white, it shone proudly in

the broiling afternoon sun. Roth had added a railing
to the porch and enclosed the area around the bottom of the house with latticework. On the porch an
old-fashioned wooden swing swayed gently, inviting
folks to sit down and talk a spell in one of the finest
and oldest country traditions.

Near the door, a bronze plaque stated that the
house had been built by Carl Unterweiss in 1923, and
resided in and maintained by his heirs until the es-
tablishment of the Dogtrot Animal Clinic by Dr.
Lawrence Roth, D.V.M. The original and current
addresses were both listed, along with the date of the
clinic opening.

The living room had been converted into a waiting area, and the adjoining dining room into an office. A chest-high counter dividing the two rooms
served as a reception desk, and Roth's receptionist,
Kathy, was manning the desk, smiling broadly as she
greeted guests and poured lemonade into paper cups.
A deli tray of sliced fruit and small, decorated cookies was on the countertop.

About twenty people, a few of them children, were
gathered in the waiting room, no great number but
an adequate crowd for the small area. Rebecca found
an unobtrusive spot in a corner and wondered where
Roth was. The sooner she saw him, complimented
the way he'd converted the house and wished him
success with his clinic, the sooner she could leave.
She had come because it was important to him that

she be there, but she was ambivalent about her decision.

Their last meeting had been frustrating for both of them, and she was resolved not to allow a similar fiasco this time. The tone of Roth's note had been friendly and sincere; if he maintained that attitude, there was a chance for friendship between them, and such a friendship would please her.

He entered the office area from what had been the kitchen in the company of a man about his own age. They were chatting easily, and their conversation was punctuated with laughter. Roth spied her in the middle of a burst of laughter and sobered immediately as their eyes locked from across the room. He said something to the man he was with, and the two of them walked toward her. Their progress was slow as Roth greeted each of his guests in passing.

When he had finally reached her, his eyes studied her face for a few seconds before he greeted her. Tilting her head slightly, she answered, "Hello, Roth." He introduced his friend as Dean Frances, his former roommate from A&M. "Dean," she said, extending her right hand.

"Rebecca is the one I told you about," Roth told his friend.

Was she imagining it, or was he consciously working at keeping his voice steady? She knew she was not imagining the significant looks passing between the two men, or Dean's frank appraisal of her as he shook her hand and said, "So you're the lady responsible for this lovely old building. What do you think of it?"

"It's charming," she said, then, looking at Roth, added, "I mean that, Roth. You've done wonders with it, yet managed to preserve the simple integrity of its design."

He stuck out his elbow. "As mastermind of this project, I think you're entitled to the deluxe guided tour."

"I wouldn't settle for anything else," she replied, looping her arm through his.

Cocking an eyebrow at his friend, Roth said, "Care to join us?"

Dean shook his head. "'Fraid not. I've already seen it, and I've got to get home. Sandy's still not a hundred per, and Eric's been a holy terror lately."

"Dean has a four-year-old and newborn at home," Roth explained.

"I'll bet there's never a dull moment at your house," Rebecca said.

"No," Dean agreed. "Sometimes I have to remind myself that these are the best years of my life. For some reason it doesn't feel that way when the baby's crying at three in the morning and I have surgery scheduled at seven."

"After all the late nights we put in at college, that should be a snap for you," Roth said.

Shaking his head, Dean said, "I'm not as young as *we* used to be."

"Speak for yourself," Roth said, laughing. "I haven't started hitting the Geritol yet!"

Dean extended his right hand. "It was great seeing you, pal. You've got an all right setup here."

"Nice guy," Rebecca said as Dean disappeared in the crowd.

"Mmm," said Roth. "He and Sandy settled in Conroe, so I don't get to see him too often."

As they made their way through the crowd, arms entwined, Rebecca was tinglingly aware of Roth's body next to hers. The chemistry between them was playing havoc with her senses again—and her resolve. *Okay,* she thought to herself, *so you'll have to take a cold shower when you get home. So what.*

"You've seen the office," he said as they passed through it. "Here's the first treatment room. Your usual stainless-steel table and cabinets with cotton balls and swabs."

"*Wood* cabinets," she said. "I'm glad you left them."

It was in what had been half of the kitchen. "My cubbyhole," he said, opening the door to the back of the former kitchen. It was small and rectangular, with a desk against one end wall and a bookcase on the other. "Can't dance in here, but at least I have a window. Keeps me from getting claustrophobic. Actually, this room's mostly for conferences. I do lab work in the surgery and most of my research at home."

They passed through the treatment room again, crossed the wide hall and stood in the doorway of what had been a bedroom. "The second treatment room. No surprises."

Roth grinned before opening the bathroom door for her. "Now this room took some creativity."

"Oh, Roth," she said, unable to stop herself from giggling. He'd papered the walls with Snoopy wallpaper, and in the bathtub, surrounded by very realistic bubbles, sat a man-size Snoopy with a bath brush in one front paw. The coup de grace, though, was the book of Garfield cartoons that lay open on a bath tray in front of the stuffed dog. "How perfect! How did you ever think of it?"

"We didn't need the bathtub, and kids seem to like it. A journalist from the *Suburbia-Reporter* came out this past Friday to do a feature on how I'm preserving an area artifact. She took several shots of Snoopy there."

"How did you make the bubbles?"

"Precisely what everyone wants to know. I tell them it's a trade secret." He leaned closer to speak confidentially. "I'll tell you, though. It's foam caulking. I got the idea when I was caulking around the windows." He sighed sensuously into her ear. "You're wearing that perfume again. By the way, I'm taking you to dinner after we close up here."

"Is that so?" she asked, trying to sound irritated by his presumption. But it was hopeless: she could feel herself softening in spite of her resolve, weakening in the face of his nearness and strength.

He surprised her by taking a step back, as though purposely trying not to crowd her. "Yes, it's so," he said lightly. "This is as much your celebration as mine. In a way, it's more uniquely yours. You gave me a house; I should be allowed to buy you dinner." Without waiting for a reply, he led her out of the bathroom and into what had been the last bedroom; now it was a surgery and laboratory. All the wire cages were empty, and Rebecca gasped softly.

"Where's Muffin?" she asked, then, with a forced calm, "Did you find her a home?"

"Mmm-hmm. A nice house with a wonderful master. It's about two hundred yards from here."

"You kept her after all?"

He smiled disarmingly. "I'm just keeping her until you change your mind about taking her. She might like living in a high rise."

Some of the all-too-familiar tension sparked between them at his mention of the high rise. Now the irritation she'd tried to muster minutes before surfaced quite easily. "Look, Roth, I came because you invited me very politely and I wanted to see what you'd done with the clinic. And I'm glad for you, really. I'll even go to dinner with you to celebrate. But you're going to have to meet me halfway to keep things on a friendly level. No more snide comments about the high rise I want to live in, please. I don't take potshots at your country estate."

He stepped back and raised his hands in the air like a movie cowboy instructed to reach for the sky, then, shrugged. The look he gave her was enough to liquefy steel. "Sorry if I offended you. Believe me, I have every intention of keeping things between us on a friendly level."

Feeling the sizzle of that heated gaze, Rebecca was far from reassured.

"It's been a nice day, and I enjoyed the dinner," Rebecca told Roth sincerely. Except for the brief, awkward moment in the laboratory, it *had* been a pleasant day, and dinner had been an unexpected treat.

"The day isn't over," he said. "The best part is upon us. I was hoping you'd stay awhile, take a look at Ginger..."

"You and that filly!" she said, laughing.

"It's my first pony," he protested. "A boy's always proud of his first pony."

"Boy indeed!" she teased.

"And you ought to give Muffin a pat, as long as you're here. She's almost fully grown now."

"You *are* a boy at heart."

"Will you stay?" When she paused, undecided, he said, "There's a full hour before sunset."

She laughed aloud. "All right. You win. But only because you've been on your best behavior." And it was true: he had been friendly and warm and polite all through dinner, never pressing for anything more than the friendship she was hoping they could share.

Ginger was prettier and friskier than ever. "How could she grow so fast?" Rebecca mused aloud.

"It's been two months since you've seen her."

"Two months? I guess it has. I hadn't realized..."

Roth had. It had been two months and three days since he'd seen Rebecca, and he had missed her every one of those days. Well, he wasn't going to go on missing her; he might be changing tactics, but he wasn't giving up on having her. He wanted her, body and mind, and he planned on having her. And she was going to come to him. "You shouldn't be such a stranger," he said lightly. He stretched his arm across her shoulders as they watched the filly, and she didn't draw away. It was a step forward.

Rebecca wasn't quite sure how it had happened. They'd been watching Ginger cavort in the small corral, and he'd put his arm across her shoulders, and then, somehow, he'd slipped his hand around her waist, and she'd been thinking she should do something about it, but all she'd done was snuggle closer to him, enjoying his masculine touch. Now they were walking to the porch, where she would sit in the glider next to him and pet Muffin and drink lemonade left over from the open house. She'd let herself be drawn into a familiar routine between them, and she didn't know why, except that she liked

Roth and enjoyed being with him. She tried, but couldn't find the harm in sitting on the porch and watching the sunset with him.

And if he kisses you? nagged an inner voice. *What then?*

Then I'll kiss him back, she told the voice. *A kiss is not a commitment. I'm only human. I enjoy a man's company. I enjoy being kissed.*

The voice countered that she wasn't playing fair, but she ignored it, and exclaimed and oohed and ahhed over how magnificent Muffin had grown as the cat met them at the screen door.

Everything happened exactly as she had anticipated. Roth brought out lemonade on a tray, then sat beside her on the glider with his arm around her while she idly stroked Muffin, who had curled up and fallen asleep in her lap.

"This is my favorite time of day," Roth reflected aloud.

"The mosquitoes would be eating us alive if the porch wasn't screened."

"You're not much of a romantic, Rebecca." His arm slid from the back of the glider to rest on her shoulders.

"No," she said, leaning her head against his shoulder. "I've never been much of a romantic."

The world that was unaffected by the future and untainted by the past was limited to his porch, the sway of the glider and the beauty of the sunset. For close to half an hour they sat there, touching but not talking, while day turned into night, and the moon took her place in the heavens. It was a full moon, round and bright. They didn't turn on the porch light, because artificial illumination would have been intrusive. The trees, stark silhouettes against the moonlight, danced in the breeze, and an orchestra of crickets commenced its evening concert.

"I'd like to make love to you in the moonlight," he said.

"If you'd kissed me instead of saying that, I'd probably have let you."

"I know that. But you would have regretted it tomorrow. Now I'll be the one with regrets," he said sadly. "I'm as stubborn about what I want as you are about what you want."

"And exactly what is it you want, Roth?"

"Your love. With no regrets."

"I think it's time I left."

"I think so, too," he agreed, his voice heavy with reluctance. She had been expecting an argument; his easy acquiescence disconcerted her. Feeling slightly rebuffed, she rose, startling Muffin with her abrupt movement. Roth put his arm across her shoulders as they walked to her car. Then, cradling her face in his palms, he said, "Thank you for coming, Rebecca."

He lowered his face to hers with infinite slowness, and the waiting amplified the effect of his kiss on her senses. She felt his warmth and the regular rhythm of his heart, smelled the woodsy cologne that his body chemistry made uniquely Roth, heard his masculine sigh of frustration as he drew away from her. For a long time, but not nearly long enough, he held her in his arms, crushing her to him, while she hugged him around the waist as though she might fade away—or cease to exist—if she did not anchor herself to him.

He relinquished contact with her by degrees, loosening his embrace, moving his hands from the small of her back to her arms, sliding them from her elbows up to her shoulders, planting light kisses on her neck, then her cheek, and finally straightening so that he was no longer touching her.

"Goodbye, Roth." Her voice was tremulous, her hands shaking as she turned to her car. He opened the door for her.

Instead of closing the door, he propped his elbow on top of the car and leaned down to look at her as she fumbled with the keys. "You made that sound very final."

"We can't go on setting ourselves up for emotional disaster, Roth."

"We're not."

"But you know it's im—"

He cut her off with a brief kiss. "There'll be other times for us, Rebecca. Wait and see." He closed the door before she could argue.

The roads that led to the freeway were abysmally dark and desolate, and even after she reached the busy, brightly lit interstate, the interior of the car remained utterly, shatteringly lonely as the gray sedan merged with the traffic and traveled east to the loop.

The Westheimer exit was crowded, as usual, and Rebecca began jockeying the car across the three lanes so she could turn toward her apartment. Then, on a whim, she gave up the maneuvering, remained in the left lane, and turned left at the corner instead of right.

She passed through the Galleria overflow—apartments, hotels, ticket offices, custom photography labs, office buildings—and then the character of the street changed subtly, from ultramodern offices to traditional houses that had been converted to picturesque shops, an open-air fruit stand, the lovely old Lanier school building. Bright lights announced that a musical revue was running at the Tower Theater. Farther up the narrow street, she passed shopping rows with nightclubs, X-rated bookstores and lingerie shops that sold fringed nighties, leather underthings, G-strings and pasties.

Finally she reached the building site she was seeking and parked across the street, double-checking that her doors were locked, and looked at the concrete and steel skeleton rising a dozen stories above the ground.

Westheimer-in-the-Sky. The first physical manifestation of an extensive plan to refurbish lower Westheimer. When Westheimer-in-the-Sky was completed, its residents would park in an electronically secured garage and enter the building under the protective eyes of a twenty-four hour security guard service.

It was the future Rebecca was facing, her destiny. She planned to live there when the building was finished, after the installation of the tall, wide windows that would afford her a spectacular view of downtown. She had called it pie in the sky, but there was no folly in a dream that could be realized. This building was steel and concrete and glass, all very tangible, of-the-earth components, and it was almost within her grasp. The commission from any of three large properties she had listed recently would make a healthy down payment on a corner unit at Westheimer-in-the-Sky.

After staring at the building for several minutes, she was startled out of her hypnoticlike trance by catcalls from two men walking past her car on the sidewalk. Stumbling past would be more accurate, because they were obviously drunk. Alarmed, Rebecca started the engine and drove off, turning toward home at the next available side street. She often drove by to check the progress on Westheimer-in-the-Sky when she had business inside the loop, but it had always been during the day.

Why she'd felt the need to see it tonight she didn't know, and she wouldn't have cared to speculate.

Chapter Ten

The Land-Com receptionist was out with a summer cold, and the agents were answering phones. "Rebecca," Phyl said from her desk, "there's a call for you on line three. Can you get it, or should I take a message?"

"I can answer it," Rebecca said. "Maybe it's a buyer for that tract on South Gessner."

"Fat chance!" said Phyl, and Rebecca had to swallow a laugh as she lifted the receiver.

"Rebecca Bruner."

"Rebecca! Aubrey Weston here."

"Aubrey, hello. What can I do for you?"

"I could give you a list, none of them related to business."

"Have you relocated yet?" she asked.

"No. Still clearing up things here in Atlanta. My place there won't be ready for another month, anyway. I really called on business. I need a favor."

"Shoot."

"Our clipping service spied the name of our corporation in that newspaper feature about the clinic—you know, the one that told how old Doc Whatzits saved the house. Your name and Land-Com's was in it, so I figured you'd seen it."

"Oh, yes," Rebecca said flatly. "Created quite a stir around here. I'm still getting calls asking me to watch out for another house."

"Our accountant seems to think that since we generated some public relations by giving the house away for restoration, the reasonable market value might be deductible. He asked me to get a statement from you as to what the reasonable market value was, so that we'll have it in our files at tax time."

"I've seen a couple of houses listed for sale, to be moved. I'll find one comparable and make out the statement. No problem."

"Thanks, Rebecca."

There was a lull in the conversation. Before it grew too awkward she said, "I hope the feature didn't cause you any embarrassment."

"None at all. We take PR where we can get it." He cleared his throat. "What's going on between you and Doc Whatzit these days?"

As always when she thought of Roth, Rebecca experienced a pang of regret. "As the song says, 'Absolutely nuthin.'"

"That's the best news I've heard all week. You're going to be hearing from me when I get to town, lady."

She hung up, wondering why the prospect of a relationship with Weston didn't excite her nearly as much as the lack of one with Roth depressed her. And the thought that she was responsible for the great nothingness and nowhereness of their relationship was the most depressing aspect of the whole dreary situation.

"Is this a slow day, or is this a slow day?" Phyl asked.

"I think it's a slow day," Rebecca said. The two women were having a cup of coffee during the lull.

"I can think of a lot of things I'd rather be doing on a beautiful Saturday than sitting here staring at phones that don't ring. You'd think people would enjoy house shopping on a day like today."

"The last weekend before school starts? They're out playing. Let's see what they're up to," Rebecca said, shuffling through the newspaper on the table in the lounge. "Here it is. 'Weekend.' Hmm. There's a golf tournament at the Houstonian. And they might be gearing up to watch the annual muscular dystrophy telethon. There's a hit musical straight off

Broadway at the Tower, and..." Her voice trailed off as she became involved with something in the paper.

"Something really special?" asked Phyl curiously.

"There's an Arabian horse show," Rebecca said distractedly, still reading. "Remember my telling you about going on a call with Roth and seeing a colt born?"

"And telling me, and telling me," Phyl said. "By your account it was the greatest miracle since the parting of the Red Sea."

Rebecca put the paper on the table in front of Phyl and pointed at a photograph. "Look at this."

Phyl read the caption aloud. "'Missy Cliburne rides her Arabian mare Classy Chassis in full Arabian costume. The costume event will be one of many at the annual Arabian Riders and Breeders Society (ARABS) show to be held at the Great Southwest Equestrian Center on Mason Road near Katy.'" She looked at Rebecca and raised an eyebrow. "So?"

"That's the mare that delivered the foal," Rebecca said.

Phyl was skeptical. "Are you sure? It wasn't that long ago. Would they have her in the ring already?"

Rebecca shrugged. "The trainer said Missy Cliburne had talked her daddy into buying the Arabians and was partial to Classy Chassis. That's her."

"Are you going to the show?"

"I don't know. I promised Kevin and Lisa I'd take them somewhere special before school starts."

"Well, do they like horses?"

Rebecca sighed exasperatedly. "Have you ever seen a kid that didn't like horses? I could take them through the stalls. There might be some ponies. . . ."

"Earth to Rebecca. Earth to Rebecca. Come in, Rebecca," Phyl teased when Rebecca's voice trailed off again.

"I was just thinking that Windborne Charlie might be there. Sometimes breeders take the foals to shows if they're for sale, or if the owner thinks the horse has potential and wants to generate interest for when they do decide to sell."

"Why don't you give that horse doctor a call and see if he wants to go with you?"

Rebecca shot Phyl a smoldering look, and Phyl held up her hands in exasperation. "It was only a suggestion."

"Roth is a closed chapter, Phyl. History."

"If you say so, Rebecca. But if that's true, I don't know why you think you have to say it so loud."

The children were enraptured by the trotting and cantering of the horses—for about twenty minutes. Lisa was the first to get fidgety, and a soft drink and popcorn from the concession stand satisfied her only for another ten minutes or so. By that time Kevin was also showing pronounced symptoms of impatience, complaining that the horses were doing the same thing over and over.

Before Rebecca could launch into a futile explanation of how each group of horses differed in age or sex, Lisa picked up Kevin's restless cue. "I want to pet the horses, Aunt Becca. You promised."

Laughing, Rebecca tweaked her niece's ponytail. "Okay, sport. Finish your drink and we'll take a walk through the stalls."

They meandered through the aisles of wooden stalls looking at the Arabians, then paused near a row of tie stalls to watch grooms brushing, saddling or unsaddling the horses in their charge.

Most owners had hung signs on the stalls to identify the horses they'd brought to show. The signs were fairly diverse in form and design, some painted by professional artists, some haphazardly scrawled, some made of wood with letters branded on that represented the ranch that owned the horse. Kevin read the names aloud as they approached each stall.

Rebecca was helping him work out an American pronunciation for an Arabian name when an unmistakable masculine voice sent shivers up her spine with the simple question, "Looking for a specific horse?"

The children rescued her from immediate comment by shouting Roth's name in unison. Roth greeted them enthusiastically, then said to Rebecca, "Classy Chassis is in the next aisle." Then, as though reading her mind, he added, "They brought Windborne Charlie, too. Classy Chassis's been creating a stir this season and they're hoping to sell Charlie for a tidy sum around the first of the year."

"Who's Charlie?" asked Lisa, hanging on to every word the adults were saying.

Roth cast Rebecca a significant look and smiled. "He's a special friend of ours. Your Aunt Rebecca and I were in the stables when he was born."

"Really?" Lisa asked, enthralled.

"Really," Rebecca confirmed. Though she spoke to the child, she was looking at Roth, her eyes held to his almost hypnotically. The special moments they'd shared in the stable on the night the colt was born seemed only seconds removed in time.

Roth said, "Let's go take a look," and Lisa responded by putting her hand in his.

Rebecca, with Kevin by her side, fell into step behind them, reluctantly acknowledging that Roth would now be a part of the group for the remainder of their stay at the horse show. Short of hustling her niece and nephew to the car and leaving, which would alarm them and prompt a lot of questions she'd rather not answer, she had no recourse but to welcome Roth as though she were as surprised and delighted to see him as the children were. But she wasn't surprised, just...strangely relieved, as though she'd been expecting him to show up, waiting for him.

Had she known, unconsciously, that there was a good chance he would be here? At the prospect, her mouth hardened and she frowned. For more than a

month she'd been trying to forget those magic moments and she'd been bombarded by reminders of
him. First there'd been the copy of the feature about
the Dogtrot Clinic that her boss had posted on the
Land-Com bulletin board. It jogged her memory
every time she walked into the office. Then Weston's call and his less-than-subtle inquiry into the
state of her relationship with Roth had brought on a
case of indigestion and a sleepless night. The photo
of Classy Chassis plastered on the front page of the
"Weekend" section of the *Chronicle* had been the
last straw.

In the press of the crowd she was practically nose
to muscle against Roth's back as he walked in front
of her; unwittingly, as she caught a whiff of his cologne, she remembered the feel of those firm back
muscles under her hands when she'd embraced him.
Oh, Roth, she thought, *why do we have to want such
different things from life?*

It was less crowded in the open space at the end of
the aisles, and Roth turned so that they could re-
group, with Rebecca and Kevin leading the way. "It's
the third stall on the left," he directed as they reached
the entry to the next row.

Kevin dashed ahead and, finding the colt's name
on a carved sign, announced, "Here he is."

"I can't see," Lisa complained, justifiably, for a
group of people was clustered around the half door
of the stall, ahhing and exclaiming over Windborne
Charlie. Roth lifted Lisa onto his shoulder to give her

a better vantage point, letting her keep the perch even after the others had moved on.

Sensing he was the star of the show, the colt alternated between striking regal poses and cavorting about the stall, kicking up his hooves and neighing as though being penned in such a small space was annoyingly tiresome for a horse of his quality. "Ooh, she's pretty," Lisa said.

"He," Kevin corrected importantly. "A colt is a boy." He put his hand inside the stall and called to the horse, who deigned to sniff it and suffer having his muzzle petted.

Rebecca and Roth exchanged amused smiles over the expression on the boy's face as the horse paid him such tribute; then, realizing the intimacy of the shared moment, Rebecca abruptly turned her head toward the stall, directing her attention to the horse in order to break eye contact with Roth.

She couldn't escape being aware of him so easily, though. He refused to let it happen and pressed his open hand against the small of her back. Yearning to lean into his touch rather than draw away from the simple gesture of possession, she exhaled raggedly, admitting defeat. He'd won a battle in a war she'd tried to avoid. It was a battle not of armies and ideals, but of individuals and emotions, and it was a very personal war.

In a movement so slight that it went unperceived by everyone but Roth and herself, she relaxed tense muscles and yielded to the overpowering temptation to lean against the strength of that open hand. And found, as she did so, that defeat is sometimes as sweet as victory.

Windborne Charlie was not as magnanimous in his attitude toward Lisa as he had been toward her brother. After nuzzling her hand, he sniffed indignantly and launched into another playful frolic around the pen. Lisa sniffed almost as indignantly as the Arabian and said, "Boy horses are dumb. Girl horses are nicer."

"They are not," Kevin said.

Laughing, Roth asked Rebecca, "Where do you stand on the colt-filly debate?"

"In the *filly*-colt debate," she said wryly, "I would say that Charlie here knows he has champion bloodlines and acts accordingly, and that a filly would behave the same under the circumstances. With a little less pomposity, perhaps."

"What's pomposity?" Lisa asked.

"It means he knows he's pretty," Rebecca answered. She dared to look at Roth. "He's imposing already, isn't he? Well on his way to becoming magnificent."

"I doubt he'll wind up a gelding," Roth said.

"What's a gelding?" Lisa said.

The panic on Roth's face was so amusing that Rebecca had to bite the inside of her cheek to stop herself laughing and making the situation worse. When she felt sufficiently in control to speak, she rescued him by saying, "A gelding is a male horse that can't become a daddy."

In the next stall, a groom was brushing Classy Chassis. "She looks none the worse for the wear of motherhood," Roth observed.

"Colt's been weaned a month," the groom volunteered. "The Cliburne girl wanted to ride Classy here in the costume event in this show. She's partial to this mare. Sits him fancy, especially in the costume event. I'd bet on blue in the finals." He grinned at them. "If bettin' was legal."

"How long before the costume event today?" Roth asked.

"I'm getting her ready now."

"We don't want to miss that," Roth said. "It's the highlight of an Arabian show. The riders wear Arabian costumes."

"Harem pants and burnooses?" Rebecca asked.

"Very elegant harem pants and burnooses. It's quite spectacular."

"I'd rather see Ginger than all these 'Rabians," Lisa interjected.

Roth knelt and helped her off his shoulder. "Maybe if you ask your Aunt Rebecca very politely, she'll bring you and Kevin by the house to see Ginger."

"Today?"

"Right after the costume event."

Lisa's face was a study of hope. "Can we, Aunt Becca?"

Rebecca hesitated. "Dr. Roth is a busy man, Lisa. He probably has lots to do this afternoon without entertaining us."

"Nonsense! I'd love to have you."

Rebecca glared at him. He wasn't playing fair, using Lisa against her. His brazen, guilty grin told her he knew that and didn't care. He was pulling out all the stops.

Kevin, feeling ignored, said, "I want to go, too, Aunt Becca. I want to see Elvira."

Mischief crept into that infuriating grin on Roth's face and into his voice. "Come on, Aunt Becca. Don't be a spoilsport. They want to see Elvira."

"Damned turkey!" Rebecca said under her breath, not necessarily referring to Elvira.

Lisa was wringing her hands. "Pleee-ase."

Grace in defeat, Rebecca thought wryly, and said, "Well, I suppose we could go by Roth's... but only for a little while."

Distracted as she was by the prospect of going back to Roth's house, Rebecca nonetheless found herself caught up in the spectacle of the costume event. The sleek Arabian horses spun a mystical, almost fairy-tale aura as they galloped around the ring, their riders' brilliantly colored capes flapping in the wind behind them. Each costume was designed to coordinate with the coloring of the horse the rider would be riding, a stunning red-and-silver burnoose for the rider of a black stallion, a bright pink-and-silver cape for the rider of a gray gelding.

Even with the stiff competition, it was easy to see why Missy Cliburne on Classy Chassis was a favorite. Missy had long thick hair almost the same color as the reddish-brown bay. She wore a bronze satin cape that flew in the wind, revealing harem pants and a halter of stunning turquoise shot through with gold. There was a wildness and a oneness about rider and horse that made them seem one, each a part of the other. The audience responded with a thundering ovation when it was announced that they had won the blue ribbon.

The roar was still subsiding when Lisa stood up and said, "It's time to go to Roth's house."

As they walked in the general direction of the parking lot, Rebecca said, "Weren't the costumes pretty?"

"I liked the stallions best," Kevin said.

"What about you, Lisa?" Roth said. "What did you think of all that finery?"

Lisa answered with a question: "Why can't a gelding be a daddy? Is it against the rules?"

His eyes telegraphed an SOS to Rebecca, but she shrugged. "She asked you."

"Yes," he told Lisa bluntly. "It's against the rules."

Chapter Eleven

Rebecca asked herself all the way to Roth's house how she'd been bamboozled into the visit. He was clever, this man with whom she'd unwittingly but irrevocably become...whatever it was she'd become with him.

What was it about him that got to her so? He wasn't pursuing her, never telephoned her, didn't show up at her doorstep. So why, why, did she feel this *pressure*? Was it because he'd said he loved her? *Or because she was afraid she was falling in love with him?*

He had arrived ahead of them and had turned Ginger out of the barn into the corral. The kids ran ahead of Rebecca, Roth helped them over the wooden fence, and, on his instruction, they began inching their way toward the filly, slowly, so as not to startle her.

Leaning casually against the fence with his arms akimbo, Roth had never looked so totally male. His eyes were fixed on her face as she approached, communicating the way he felt about her in a language as old as love itself. They did not exchange words of greeting because words would have been superfluous. Rebecca simply stepped into place beside him, and he put his arms across her shoulders as they watched the children play with the pony.

After a while, she said, "Did you know I'd be there today?"

"I was hoping you would. I thought you might if you saw the photo in the newspaper." He had edged closer to her, and she leaned against him, drawing from the strength of his lean body. He said, "It's been lonely here without you, Rebecca. The moonlight . . . I don't know . . . seems empty."

"I don't belong here."

"Are you sure of that?"

"Not when you're holding me like this."

"Then I'll have to hold you like this more often. I'd hold you like this forever if I could."

Eventually Kevin tired of playing with the pony and asked to see Elvira. Rebecca and Roth followed the children to the poultry pen, and he took feed from the storage room so that the kids could feed the chicks, who were now adult hens. Elvira, whose tail feathers reached to Lisa's shoulders, was the hit of the day.

"You guys think she'll be fat enough to eat by Thanksgiving?" Roth asked lightly.

Lisa was horror-stricken. "You're going to *eat* Elvira?"

Roth ruffled the child's hair. "No, darling. I couldn't butcher her."

"Some farmer you are," Rebecca said under her breath.

The look he shot at her was significant. "I never claimed to be a farmer. I'm a veterinarian." He put his arm across Kevin's shoulders. "I've been thinking of getting a tom turkey and letting Elvira here raise a brood. I might build a separate pen for the turkeys up next to the office so that the kids who bring their animals here could look out the window and see real live turkeys. What do you think of that?"

"I think it would be neat," Kevin said.

"So do I," piped in Lisa.

"Then I'll have to do it. Do you suppose I could get your Aunt Becca to help me find a tom for Elvira?"

"Oh, sure," said Kevin. "Aunt Becca knows all about turkeys."

"I certainly do," Rebecca muttered, and was ignored.

Eventually Roth suggested to the kids that they go into the coop to gather eggs. As soon as they were out of earshot, he looked at Rebecca. "I meant that about not being a farmer. I'm not a farmer, and I'm not looking for a farm wife to help with the plowing and see to the canning."

"What are you looking for?" she asked, regretting the question as she asked it.

His thumb grazed her cheek. "A lover. A friend. A partner."

"You want children." It came out like an accusation.

He grinned guiltily. "Only a couple. When the time is right."

She said it again; she'd lost track of the number of times she'd said it, aloud to him, silently to herself. At the moment, she was no more sure of it than he. "I'm not the woman for you, Roth."

He grabbed her by the arms. "You can say that until your voice gives out. You can deny that what exists between us exists, but nothing changes, Rebecca. I love you." With a miserable groan, he released her. His voice was soft but intense. "If I thought you'd be happy living in an ivory tower—"

"We found a bunch of eggs!" The children were crossing the chicken yard toward them. "We can't carry them all."

"There's a basket in the coop," Roth said. "I'll get it for you."

Rebecca sagged against a fence post and shuddered involuntarily, shell-shocked by the exchange the children had interrupted. How could they have been having such a conversation in a chicken yard? It was ludicrous—as ludicrous as the fact that she was still in that chicken yard, leaning against a fence post, trembling like a frightened child while Roth had walked calmly off to gather eggs with the children.

Gradually she regained her composure. Two, perhaps three minutes passed before the children came bursting from the coop again carrying wire baskets. "We found nine eggs," Kevin said. "Dr. Roth says we can make omelets."

"He's going to show us how to cook them, and he's going to let us break them," Lisa added.

Rebecca sighed under her breath. He'd done it again. He'd made the kids another offer she couldn't refuse.

"If I didn't know better, I'd think you'd planned this," she told Roth later in the kitchen. Baked beans were simmering on the stove, the children were beating eggs, she was grating cheese and Roth was carving a ham that just happened to be in his refrigerator.

"A bachelor has to be prepared for any eventuality."

"Uh-huh," she said skeptically.

"You guys going to pitch some horseshoes after dinner?" Roth asked when they were all gathered around the kitchen table.

"We won't have time," Rebecca said quickly. "I've got to get the kids home. My sister—"

"Mommy and Daddy are going out, 'member, Aunt Becca?" Lisa said.

"They're going to a dinner theater," Kevin informed Roth. "Aunt Becca's baby sitting."

"Then you can stay," Roth said.

Rebecca laid down her fork and squared her shoulders as she glared at him across the table. "School opens Tuesday, and the kids have to get on a schedule. They absolutely, positively have to be home, bathed and in bed by nine o'clock."

With irritating calm, Roth consulted the clock on the wall and then his wristwatch. "It's five forty-five. If you leave by seven-thirty, you should have the kids home in plenty of time. That gives you an hour...almost two hours."

The matter was settled. Content, the children resumed their eating. Rebecca frowned at Roth and picked up her fork. When Roth raised his eyebrows, feigning innocence, and grinned back at her, she battled a powerful urge to kick his shin under the table.

Never short of surprises, Roth ferreted tin-roof ice cream out of his freezer for dessert. "I suppose," Rebecca said, "you just happen to have a weakness for tin-roof ice cream?"

"My closet vice," he confessed. "All those calories and chocolate and cholesterol. I suffer guilt with every delectable spoonful."

The children finished their ice cream quickly and were impatient to get outside again. Rebecca gathered the dessert dishes and carried them to the sink.

Roth walked up behind her and slid his arms around her waist. "Leave them. I'll do them later."

"The pot and skillet I'll leave for later. The dishes I'm going to rinse and stack in the dishwasher while you set up the horseshoes for the kids."

He pressed his chin cozily into her shoulder and whispered into her ear, "I was hoping you'd come with me to the barn."

"Oh, no," she said. "I went with you to get the horseshoes once, remember?"

Nuzzling his cheek against her neck, he said, "Mmm. That's why I was hoping you'd go with me again."

"Nothing doing, Romeo." She pried his arms from around her. "Go on. The kids are waiting for you to set up their game."

Frowning, he stepped back to give her some space. "Bossy, aren't you?"

"Just tired of being manipulated."

He winced. "I guess I deserved that. I don't deny that I've been a bit manipulative today."

"A bit?"

"If you want me to say I'm sorry, I'm not. I did what I had to do to get you here and keep you here long enough for the two of us to discuss our relationship."

"We don't have a relationship to discuss, Roth. The longer you refuse to face that fact—"

The back door slammed, small feet thundered through the hall toward the kitchen, young voices called Roth's name through winded giggles. The children bounded into the room. "We want to play horseshoes!"

"Yeah. We want to play horseshoes!"

Rebecca was struck, touched, by the patience, the affection, in Roth's smile. "Then I guess I'd better get the horseshoes, huh?"

They were pulling at him, bouncing around his heels like hound pups around an old momma dog, and Roth loved it. Rebecca's heart swelled with tenderness for that part of his nature. She blinked back tears as she forced her attention to the dishes in the sink. A man like Roth deserved whatever it was he was yearning for. She felt a stab of regret that she was not the woman who could give it to him.

The entire time Rebecca worked at the sink, Muffin walked to and fro, meowing and brushing against her legs and nudging her ankles with her nose. When she had finished with the dishes, Rebecca dried her hands and picked up the cat. "Spoiled rotten, aren't you? I wouldn't put it past Roth to share his tin-roof ice cream with you."

She carried the cat to the porch and sat down on the glider. Muffin remained in her lap and soon curled up and fell asleep.

Roth had driven the stakes for horseshoe pitching and was playing with the children. As soon as he spied Rebecca on the porch, he nodded and immediately extricated himself from the game. Rebecca tensed as he approached, steeling herself for the imminent confrontation.

He did not sit down after entering the screened enclosure of the porch, but leaned against the doorjamb and regarded her appraisingly. "I've done a lot of thinking since the last time you were here," he said without preamble. "A lot of soul-searching and self-examination."

There was nothing to say. Silence stretched between them until he resumed the one-sided conversation. "I understand you, Rebecca...where you come from, what you went through, why you want what you want. And I've tried to pinpoint what it is I can offer you to compensate for that high rise with a view." He studied his hands for a moment, hands that were finely formed, strong, skilled in healing, capable of great gentleness. "I'm not a wealthy man, Rebecca, not one of the movers and shakers that make the city tick."

His eyes met hers and impressed her with their sincerity. "I love you, Rebecca. That's all I can offer. Love and security. But—and I've thought about this—I think in the end that would be enough for you. Otherwise, I wouldn't be telling you this. I'd let you go."

Had it not been for the cat sleeping in her lap, Rebecca would have gone to him, comforted him, but all she could do was say his name miserably.

"Don't," he said, an edge of pain in his voice. "Please don't ask me to stop until I've finished." He closed the distance between them, sat down beside her, and, with a crooked forefinger under her chin, guided her face toward his. "I know that if you walk out of my life for good, you'll get that condo and sooner or later you'll meet a mover and shaker who has a penthouse even higher in the sky and closer to town. And the person you want to become will be happy."

"The person I want to become?"

"Yes. The antithesis of shy, plain little Becky Bruner. Her opposite. She knows exactly what she wants and goes after it. And she gets it, no matter what she gives up along the way."

"You don't think I'm that person already?"

"No. Because that's not the person you are, Rebecca, any more than timid Becky was. The real you lies somewhere between the two extremes. There's a warm, wonderful person inside you with nothing to prove. That's the person you were meant to be. And that woman could be happy with a man like me. Because you'll find richer men and more powerful men, and they'll love you in their way, but you'll only be a part of the larger-than-life existence they live."

Throwing his arms around her, he drew her to him and hugged her urgently, as though afraid that if he let go of her, some catastrophe would befall them both. Muffin skittered off her lap at her sudden movement, as she twisted toward him.

"You'll never find another man to love you with a higher quality of love than mine," he said intensely. "Love would be at the center of my life, of our lives together, not relegated to the periphery. If you're the person I think you are, a love like that could compensate for a view of downtown."

Gradually he loosened his embrace until one arm was around her and the other hand held hers in his lap. "Can you settle for that quality of love, Rebecca?"

Threading her fingers through his, she drew his hand to her lips and kissed his knuckles, one by one. "I don't know. But I do know that I could never be loved by a finer man than you, Roth. The movers and the shakers are compromisers, and you're not. You've got too much integrity for compromise."

"And you," he said. "How are you on compromise?"

She sighed, softly and sadly. "I'm not sure I have enough confidence for it."

The rest of the world went on as usual. The children got tired of pitching horseshoes and Roth showed them Snoopy in the clinic bathtub.

When it was time to go, they said goodbye to the animals and thanked Roth for inviting them. Roth hugged each of them, kissed Rebecca briefly on the lips and helped her make sure their seat belts were fastened properly. Then he watched sadly as her car became a dot in the distance and disappeared, wondering if he'd ever see her again.

Rebecca was wondering the same thing.

Chapter Twelve

So you really did it?" Phyl said, pouring fresh coffee into the mug she kept perpetually full.

"At nine-thirty on the dot."

"Well?" urged Phyl. "Elucidate. Emote. How does it feel to be a woman of property?"

"Earnest money does not a property owner make." Rebecca picked up her own mug of coffee, looked inside, frowned and set it back on the table.

"What gives?" Phyl asked. "I would have thought you'd be elated."

"I would have thought the same thing, but I just feel—I don't know—numb. I guess it's just overwhelming. I mean, earnest money is the simple part. Just sign a contract and hand them a check. But I think about committing myself to a mortgage payment for thirty years—that's longer than I've been alive."

Phyl rolled her eyes. "Ah, to be thirty again!" She sat down opposite Rebecca. "You know, there aren't many single women who manage to buy property before they're thirty. You must be proud of yourself."

"Lucky is more the word for it. I've been lucky with listings and sales, especially lately. If it weren't for having the money from Daddy's property to fall back on in a squeeze, I'd be wary of committing myself to a hefty mortgage payment. It would be like banking on luck."

Deep in thought, she tapped the tabletop with her fingernails in an erratic rhythm. "It's ironic that the money we got for the farm should be a form of security for me now."

Phyl studied her friend's face. "Ironic how?"

Rebecca shook her head and shrugged. She lived in the present and was not accustomed to sharing anything about her past. Taking a deep breath, she continued, "It's just...I guess when I was growing up, I never felt we had anything that would be worth anything to anybody else."

"Land is an investment. We tell people that all the time in our business."

Rebecca sighed. "I just never thought of that farm as *that kind* of land. And certainly never as an investment."

"'The grass is always greener' concept," Phyl mused. "Or 'not seeing the forest for the trees.' Funny how old clichés hit so close to the target."

"That's how they become clichés."

"I suppose. So when do I get to see Westheimer-in-the-Sky?"

"They're having the official ribbon cutting next Thursday. Cocktails and open house for residents and the press. I could show you my condo then if you'd like to go."

Phyl considered the invitation a moment. "Dave's flying to Dallas on Wednesday."

"Again?" Rebecca asked.

"Uh-huh. If I couldn't see how immersed he is in this merger when he's home, I'd think he had a mistress stashed up in the 'Big D.'"

"You know Dave better than that."

"You bet. He's married to his job. I'm the only mistress he has time for." Her voice revealed that an old wound was still tender.

You'll find richer men and more powerful men, and they'll love you in their way, but you'll only be a part of the larger-than-life existence they live. Roth's words. Dave was a corporate attorney, a mover and shaker, and his marriage to Phyl was only one part of his larger-than-life existence. Roth would be a family man.

Rebecca sighed once again. Why couldn't she stop thinking about him? She had closed that book, hadn't she? Didn't today prove that she knew what she wanted? He'd given her pause. She'd done some soul-searching of her own after his love talk, especially after the South Gessner property sold and she knew she could buy the condo. In the end she'd put down the earnest money. She wouldn't have been able to take such a step if she weren't sure it was what she wanted. *Or would you?* she wondered, a frown creasing her brow. She thought she'd dealt with all the lingering doubts.

"About Thursday..." Phyl interrupted Rebecca's train of thought. "Sounds like a lot more fun than sitting in front of the television stuffing my face. Are you sure you want to drag me along? I mean, if you'd rather take a date..."

"I checked. Mel Gibson's washing his hair that night."

"Rebecca!" Phyl admonished in a tone she might have used with her children, the youngest of whom was a junior in high school.

"I want you to see my condo, Phyl. And the sales rep almost begged me to bring some fellow agents with me. 'We're always anxious to show off Westheimer-in-the-Sky to real estate professionals,' and all that cock-and-bull."

Phyl threw up her hands in acquiescence. "What can I say? If Mel Gibson's busy, why not?"

"Good," Rebecca said. "It's a date."

"I'll expect a corsage," Phyl said dryly.

"May I see your driver's license and invitation?" Rebecca produced both documents for the uniformed guard, and he logged her name and license number on a time card, which he validated in a punch clock.

"I'll need yours, too, ma'am," he said to Phyl, and added her name to the card before raising the striped arm that blocked their passage into the Westheimer-in-the-Sky parking garage.

The procedure in the lobby was much the same—identification, verification, documentation. The guard filed their names and went back to watching the TV monitor that scanned the parking garage.

"I feel as though we're entering the high-security research facility," Phyl said after the two women had been allowed through the door into the inner lobby and had punched the Up button on the elevator. "Is getting out as difficult as getting in?"

"It's called security, Phyl. Have you watched the news lately? There are people out there who hurt other people and steal things from nice places like this."

"I suppose it's better to be secure than victimized," Phyl said without conviction, "but I feel peculiar having to show identification and everything, like I'm ... *suspect* in some way.''

"It's a shame that society's so messed up that decent people have to live behind locked doors.''

"Hey," said Phyl, zeroing in on Rebecca's morosity. "I didn't mean to rain on your parade. Once you move in and the guards know you, I'm sure they'll just nod politely and say, 'Howdy,' when you come in.''

Rebecca nodded. "I imagine so. Residents have computer-encoded cards for the gate monitor in the parking lot.''

If Phyl's reaction to Westheimer-in-the-Sky's tight security had been negative, her reaction to the first sight of the party room was predictably positive. Glass walls, a glossy quarry tile floor in a checkerboard pattern, and sleek furniture with uncluttered lines in accent colors combined to convey a mixture of contemporary flash and understated elegance. She whistled under her breath. "Fan-cy.''

"The style to which I plan to become accustomed," Rebecca said dully. She expected to feel a surge of excitement as the reality of having her condo sank in, but nothing seemed to relieve this ... this numbness.

"Give me five minutes and I could become accustomed to it, too," Phyl said. "Maybe when the kids are out of school and on their own, Dave and I will sell our piece of suburbia and rejoin the hep set.''

"*Hep* set?"

Phyl shrugged. "Before your time. It means the with-it crowd. But I suppose that's before your time, too."

"I get the drift," Rebecca said. "Oh, here comes Vanessa, the sales rep. Prepare to be drooled over." She made the necessary introductions, and Vanessa drooled, as anticipated, over the fact that a real estate agent was in attendance.

"Be sure and visit our open model, one floor down," she told Phyl, then said to Rebecca, "If you'd like to show Phyl your unit, I'll leave word at the desk to release the key."

"I'd appreciate that," Rebecca said.

"Consider it taken care of," Vanessa said, and excused herself to greet some new arrivals.

"Accommodating, isn't she? I see what you mean about her," Phyl said.

"Sales is the name of her game."

"And she plays to win," Phyl said cryptically. "Let's go see what kind of table this outfit sets."

An ice sculpture shaped like Westheimer-in-the-Sky stood at the center of the long table, surrounded by a plethora of party fare: miniature cream puffs filled with meat salad, sliced fruits with dill dip, assorted chips and fancy crackers, sliced meats and cheeses with party rye, bite-size cookies and petits fours. "I'm glad we decided to eat *after* this shindig," Phyl said, picking up a salmon-colored paper plate and a napkin with the Westheimer-in-the-Sky logo printed on it in gold letters.

"You know, Rebecca," she said later, between bites, "I can't help noticing that I'm more enthused about all this than you are."

"I'm enthused," Rebecca said defensively.

Phyl cast her a skeptical look. "If this is enthused, I'd hate to see you in low gear. Look at that beige dress. Isn't it sharp? I'll bet it's a hundred percent silk."

"At least," said Rebecca. The man next to the woman wearing the beige dress under discussion reminded her of Roth, except that his features were not as well defined as Roth's, his shoulders were not quite as broad, and his hands, as he gestured, didn't look nearly as strong and agile as Roth's.

A frown settled on Rebecca's face. Damn it, why was Roth constantly on her mind? She hadn't even talked to him since he'd poured his heart out to her at his house.

"Champagne, ladies?" A uniformed waiter placed a silver tray of stemmed glasses within their reach.

"Just the person I've been waiting for," Phyl said, and took a glass.

Rebecca picked up a glass without comment and sipped the champagne. She had thought of calling Roth to let him know she'd put down earnest money on the condo, then had discarded the idea. What, after all, would she say? *Just in case you're wonder-*

*ing, I've bought a condo, so I won't be needing the
love you offered me.*

"How 'bout showing me through the model after
we finish our food?" Phyl asked.

"Sure."

"If you see Dave, tell him hello for me."

Rebecca blinked to attention. "I thought Dave was
in Dallas."

"He is," Phyl said wryly. "I thought maybe that's
where you were."

Rebecca's shoulders drooped as she exhaled. "I'm
sorry, Phyl. I know I'm not good company."

Phyl's face registered her concern. "Are you okay,
honey?"

"I'm just feeling a little punk."

"Female trouble?"

Rebecca shook her head. "Wrong time of the
month."

"Man trouble?"

The image of Roth's face flashed through Rebecca's mind. "No," she lied, not wanting to try to explain what she herself hadn't sorted out.

"Well, if you ever need to talk..."

Rebecca forced a smile. "Thanks, Phyl, but I
couldn't put it into words. It must be premortgage
jitters. I've heard clients mention them. From now
on I'll know what they're talking about."

"Is this the same floor plan as yours?" Phyl asked as they entered the model.

"No. This is the standard two bedroom. The corner units have a small study."

Phyl looked around at the decorator-coordinated room. "Nice. The living room is larger than I anticipated. What's the kitchen like?"

"It's a one-cook kitchen," Rebecca said, leading the way. "Small but adequate, with built-in appliances, including a microwave."

Phyl giggled. "You can sure tell we're real estate agents. We're talking about the kitchen the way doctors would discuss a patient's diseased liver."

"Let's go check out the gallstones in the master bedroom," Rebecca said.

The master was an interior room, and the decorator had compensated for the lack of windows with a garden mural on one wall and a floor-to-ceiling mirror panels on another. Both were marked unobtrusively with a tiny card that read, in fine script, "Decorator item. Not included."

"As I live and breathe! It's Rebecca Bruner."

Rebecca turned toward the male voice. "Aubrey? What are you doing here?"

"I *live* here," he said. "Or I will when I get unpacked. The moving van just pulled out an hour ago." He seemed to notice Phyl for the first time and stuck out his right hand. "Aubrey Weston."

"Phyllis Jacobs," Phyl said, giving Rebecca a "what the hell?" look as she shook his hand.

"Phyl is an associate of mine at Land-Com," Rebecca said to Aubrey. Then to Phyl, "Aubrey's the one who bought that property near Katy. You know, the one who let Dr. Roth have the house for the clinic."

"I gave *you* the house, Rebecca. You gave it to the good Dr. Roth," Aubrey corrected. There was a predatory, almost challenging gleam in his eye as he looked at her. "So, are you ladies here in a professional capacity?"

"Rebecca put down earnest money on a condo here. I came to see it," Phyl explained.

Aubrey lifted Rebecca's hand and placed it on his arm, trapping it there with his hand. "Neighbors? Now I know I'm going to like living in Houston. What level are you on?"

"Seventh."

Aubrey smiled broadly. "I'm in seven hundred."

"On the next corner?" Rebecca was startled into speaking her thought.

"Small world," Aubrey said, and abandoned her hand to stretch his arm across her shoulder. "You know," he said to Phyl, "calling Rebecca was on my list of things to do tomorrow morning. I didn't have her home number or I would have tried calling her tonight. Then I decided to see what was going on at the open house, and I looked up and here she is. That's an omen, don't you think?"

"Yes. Undoubtedly. An omen," said Phyl. He didn't know her well enough to catch the irony in her agreement, but Rebecca heard it and knew that Phyl had sensed her lack of interest in Aubrey's advances.

"Why don't we go back up to the party room for a glass of champagne?" he suggested.

"Phyl hasn't seen the model yet," Rebecca said.

The hint bounced off thick skin. "Then let's show it to her."

"Where do you get these hunks? I mean, they just seem to drift into your life. Is he really trying to get you to teach aerobics at his gym?" They were back upstairs in the ladies' room across the hall from the party room.

"You've got to help me, Phyl. Back me up on this. I do *not* want to go to dinner with him. He's trying to use your acquiescence against me."

"He's not taking no for an answer, Rebecca. Is it that big a deal? We were planning to go somewhere after the party anyway, and he's going to have to eat by himself if we don't go with him."

"Oh, Phyl, don't be naive. Your motherly instinct is showing. That man has never eaten a meal alone in his life."

"What gives with you, Rebecca? What do you have against gorgeous men?"

Rebecca sighed in exasperation. "I'm just not in the mood for Aubrey Weston tonight."

"All right. All right. I'll say I just remembered that Trace has a test tomorrow and I need to get home and make sure he studies."

Relieved, Rebecca said, "Thanks, Phyl. I won't forget it."

"What would you do if I weren't with you?"

"Probably resort to karate."

"The man owns a gym, for Pete's sake," Phyl said. "Don't try anything physical."

"Physical is what I intend to avoid with him. At least until..." Until she forgot Roth?

"Until what?"

Rebecca blinked. "I don't know. Until I shake this mood. I'm not sure it would be a good idea to get involved with a neighbor, anyway. If it went sour, I'd have to keep avoiding him in the halls and elevators."

"That's the most sensible thing you've said all night. Well, we'd better get back or he'll wonder if we slipped down a drain."

"I wouldn't put it past him to come charging in with a plunger to rescue us."

Phyl put her hand on Rebecca's arm. "Rebecca?"

"Huh?"

"Lighten up, okay? This is a concerned friend talking. You're wound up tighter than a spring."

Rebecca nodded.

Aubrey was near the door to the party room, talking to a generously endowed woman wearing a dress with a neckline cut low enough to display most of her assets. She had a long mass of curly blond hair that reminded Rebecca of one of Dolly Parton's wigs. "See what I mean," Rebecca said under her breath.

He greeted them broadly and solicitously introduced them to Udora Damon. "Udora's another neighbor," she said.

"Six-oh-five," she volunteered.

"Udora's husband is in Denver."

"We commute between here and there. Naturally, when we decided to get a condo here, I got stuck with furnishing it and putting it all together."

"How droll," Phyl said dryly.

"Absolutely," Udora agreed. "It's so bor-ing waiting on telephone men and furniture trucks. I'm so glad they had this party to relieve the doldrums."

"Udora just asked if I knew of a place in the area that delivers decent food, and I told her we were going out and suggested she tag along with us."

"I can't tell you how delightful it's going to be to have someone to eat with for a change. We have friends in town, of course, but a person can only impose on hospitality so long."

"I'm afraid," said Phyl with the appropriate dose of regret, "that it'll have to be a party of two. I just remembered that my son asked me to help him with his history tonight."

"It's still early," Aubrey said. "Couldn't he wing it until you get there?"

"It's his worst subject, and he's trying to get off to a strong start. And he's so exhausted after football practice that he crashes around nine. It's now or never."

Aubrey's left arm snaked around Rebecca's waist. "You'll still go with us, won't you?"

"She drove," Phyl said quickly. "So—"

"We'll drive you home on the way to dinner."

"It's too far out of your way, Aubrey, and that would put me driving home alone late tonight. I'm afraid we're going to have to pass. There'll be other times."

He hugged her and whispered, "Count on it, sugar."

"Too bad," said Udora, unconvincingly feigning disappointment. "I was hoping to get to know you better." She put her hand on Aubrey's free arm. "I guess that leaves us. If you still want to go."

"Oh, of course," said Aubrey. "No sense in both of us eating alone."

Rebecca ducked from under Aubrey's arm and, looking at Phyl, said, "If we're going to see my condo and get you home in time to help Trace, I'm afraid . . ." She looked from Aubrey to Udora. "If you'll excuse us . . ."

"Whew!" she said as soon as they were in the hall. "We made it. You were a champ, Phyl."

"Champion liar."

"Champion friend," Rebecca corrected. "I couldn't have borne dinner with Aubrey, let alone Goldilocks."

"She didn't seem so bad," Phyl said. "Obvious but harmless."

"Her false eyelashes practically brushed her shoulders when she blinked."

"Are you jealous or what?" Phyl said.

"Not jealous. Just . . ." Her voice trailed off, and the rest of her sentence was lost as the elevator door opened and they stepped inside.

Vanessa had left word at the desk as promised. The guard gave Rebecca the key to her condo without a hassle, and they took the elevator back up to the seventh floor.

Outside, the sun had begun its descent, the streetlamps had been turned on by light sensors and motorists on the nearby freeway were switching on their headlights. Through the twilight, the view from the living room was festive. Phyl and Rebecca walked to the window. "I'm speechless," Phyl said. "It's breathtaking. If I lived here, I'd run from window to window just seeing what's going on outside."

"I plan to do just that." She turned her head to face Phyl. "Do you want a guided tour?"

"Not unless you just feel like showing me around. I'm used to wandering."

While Phyl started her wandering in the kitchen and dining room, Rebecca went to the master bedroom and looked out the window there. Here was where she would lie in bed and watch the city in action if she chose. Far in the distance were tall buildings with lit and unlit windows forming irregular checkerboard patterns in the deepening twilight. Closer in was the freeway with its clog of evening commuters.

Rebecca did a double take of the freeway. Traffic was at a standstill in one of the outbound lanes, and cars were backed up beyond the field of vision allowed by the window. Looking more carefully, she saw that there had been a collision and two disabled automobiles were causing the bottleneck. The shrill wail of a siren drew her attention just as the blinking strobe light of a police car caught her eye. It was moving up the shoulder toward the accident scene, trailed by an ambulance and two wreckers.

People were milling around the crippled cars. From her perch in the sky, Rebecca could see hands gesturing as the newly arrived officers conversed with drivers and witnesses. She had a bird's-eye view, too, of the officers as they urgently summoned the ambulance attendants to one of the cars, and of the attendants pulling an unconscious passenger from the backseat. She watched transfixed as the injured person was loaded into the ambulance. Then the ambulance departed with its siren wailing, and the wrecker drivers pulling their trucks up to the cars and began preparing them for towing.

Suddenly she felt sick to the stomach. Was this the view she'd been waiting for, the action she'd yearned to be part of? Was it for this that she had carelessly discounted the love of a good man and a fulfilling one-to-one relationship?

"Did I hear sirens?" Phyl's wandering had brought her to the bedroom.

"There was an accident on the freeway."

Both women stared out the window, their eyes fixed on the panorama outside, but their thoughts at that moment were vastly different. "Forgive me for being a bit envious," Phyl said. "You've really made it, Rebecca. You're single, attractive, independent, with a hunk for a neighbor and a window at the top of the world."

Rebecca's voice was eerily flat and expressionless. "Ironic, isn't it?"

Phyl turned her head and studied her friend's face. "What's ironic?"

"That I've finally made it and I don't like the view."

Phyl touched Rebecca's cheek and found it clammy. "Honey, are you all right?"

"No. I'm not all right. I'm all wrong." She turned to face her friend. "But I think I could be all right." The animation was back in her voice. In fact there was an urgency, an excitement in her manner. "Would you mind terribly if we left and didn't go to dinner?"

"No, honey, but if you're not feeling well—"

Rebecca smiled disarmingly. "But I am well. Or at least I will be as soon as... I feel as though an enormous weight has been lifted from my shoulders. How much do you think this building weighs, Phyl? That's how much lighter I am. Come on, let's get away from this albatross."

"You only had one champagne," Phyl said, running to keep up with Rebecca's flight from the condominium. "You aren't taking something that would react with alcohol, are you? Diet pills or decongestants?"

"Don't be ridiculous."

"Maybe you'd like to go upstairs for another drink?" Phyl suggested. "I could abstain, and drive you home."

"I'm thirsty," Rebecca said, "but not for champagne. You don't mind stopping at the supermarket on the way to the office, do you?"

"Hell, no. I'm just along for the ride. And it's turning out to be a doozy."

Rebecca stopped in midstep. "Did you say something?"

"I said, 'Trace has probably wiped us out of peanut butter, Ritz crackers and milk. I'd love to go to the market.'"

Getting out of Westheimer-in-the-Sky proved to be much easier than getting in, and they were soon at a store. They used one cart, into which Phyl tossed breakfast cereal, crackers, peanut butter, milk, a six-pack of imported beer, a plastic pot scraper, a package of cinnamon rolls and a four-pack of toilet paper. Rebecca put in only one item.

"That's all you're getting?" Phyl asked.

"All I need," Rebecca said with a Cheshire cat smile.

"For what?"

"Forever."

Phyl shook her head as though she'd been rattled by a loud explosion and raced behind Rebecca to the car. In the office parking lot, she loaded her groceries into her own car and told Rebecca, "I have mixed feelings about letting you drive off in the state you're in."

"The only state I'm in is one of euphoria."

"Are you sure you—"

"I'm fine, Phyl. Really. I've... There's just something I've got to do, that's all." She dispelled Phyl's questioning look with, "I'll tell you all about it tomorrow, I promise. I'll..." She hesitated. "I'll have the end of the story by then."

After waiting to be sure that Phyl's car started, Rebecca drove to the freeway and, from there, to Roth's house. A floodlamp illuminated the clinic, but the front of the house was dark. For a moment she experienced a jolt of panic, fearing Roth wasn't at home, until she spied his truck near the barn. And then she saw the light coming from the living-room window at the side of the house and heaved a sigh of relief.

The porch door was unlocked, and she went directly to the door of the house and beat on it. Hadn't he heard her car on the drive? It was perhaps a minute before he answered her knock, quite possibly the longest single minute in her entire lifetime. He was in his stocking feet, his hair was ruffled and his eyes were glazed by recent sleep.

He blinked at the sight of her, disbelieving, and said, "Rebecca."

"Were you sleeping? Did I wake you up?"

He was kneading the back of his neck with his fingers. "I must have dozed off. I had early surgery this morning."

Suddenly the enormity of what she was doing descended upon Rebecca, and all she could say was, "I didn't mean to wake you up."

He stepped aside, inviting her in, and smiled. "It's all right. I was dreaming about you anyway."

"Were you drinking lemonade?"

"No. But dreams can be amended."

"You don't know how aware of that I am at this moment." She held out the brown grocery bag she was holding. "I was...somewhere...and I suddenly got thirsty for homemade lemonade."

He took the bag, peered inside, pulled out the plastic bag of lemons. "Then let's make some."

"Roth."

He had started toward the kitchen, and he turned to find her standing there with her arms outstretched. In a single stride he reached her and drew her to him, and his lips lowered hungrily over hers. Throwing her arms around him, she clung to him with a strength that startled them both. He kissed her lips, her cheeks, her neck, and whispered her name in entreaty. "Tell me that you've come to stay."

"Yes," she said with a sound that was half laughter, half sob. "I almost made a terrible mistake, but I'm here now. It was so close, Roth. I actually put earnest money down on that high rise." She cocked her head and smiled at him through tears of happiness. "It cost me two hundred dollars to find out what I don't want. And what I do."

He wiped tears from her cheeks with his thumbs. "Are you sure?"

She sniffed. "Yes, Roth. I'm sure."

He looked at her adoringly, tear tracks and all. "Don't you think it's about time you called me Larry?"

"Oh, Larry, I love you!" she said, and nestled her cheek against his chest.

"I love you, too, Becca."

"Becca?" she asked against his chest.

"What the children call you. You were always yourself with them. Not Becky, timid and shy, not Rebecca, cool and unyielding. Becca, warm and strong and capable of loving."

Her arms tightened around him. "Will you always call me that, Larry?"

He hugged her closer still and kissed the top of her head. "Forever, darling Becca. Forever."

Take 4 Silhouette Romance novels
FREE

Then preview 6 brand-new Silhouette Romance® novels—delivered to your door as soon as they are published—for 15 days without obligation. When you decide to keep them, pay just $1.95 each, *with no shipping, handling or other charges of any kind!*

Each month, you'll meet lively young heroines and share in their thrilling escapades, trials and triumphs...virile men you'll find as attractive and irresistible as the heroines do...and colorful supporting characters you'll feel you've always known.

Start with 4 Silhouette Romance novels absolutely FREE. They're yours to keep without obligation, and you can cancel at any time.

As an added bonus, you'll also get the Silhouette Books Newsletter FREE with every shipment. Every issue is filled with news on upcoming books, interviews with your favorite authors, even their favorite recipes.

Simply fill out and return the coupon today!
This offer is not available in Canada.

Silhouette Romance®

Silhouette Books, 120 Brighton Rd., P.O. Box 5084, Clifton, NJ 07015-5084

**Clip and mail to: Silhouette Books,
120 Brighton Road, P.O. Box 5084, Clifton, NJ 07015-5084**

YES. Please send me 4 Silhouette Romance novels FREE. Unless you hear from me after I receive them, send me six new Silhouette Romance novels to preview each month as soon as they are published. I understand you will bill me just $1.95 each (a total of $11.70) with no shipping, handling, or other charges of any kind. There is no minimum number of books that I must buy, and I can cancel at any time. The first 4 books are mine to keep.   **BR18L6**

Name	(please print)

Address	Apt. #

City	State	Zip

Terms and prices subject to change. Not available in Canada.
SILHOUETTE ROMANCE is a service mark and registered trademark.   SR-SUB-1

FOUR UNIQUE SERIES
FOR EVERY WOMAN YOU ARE ...

Silhouette Romance

Heartwarming romances that will make you laugh and cry as they bring you all the wonder and magic of falling in love.

Silhouette Special Edition

Expanded romances written with emotion and heightened romantic tension to ensure powerful stories. A rare blend of passion and dramatic realism.

Silhouette Desire

Believable, sensuous, compelling—and above all, romantic—these stories deliver the promise of love, the guarantee of satisfaction.

Silhouette Intimate Moments

Love stories that entice; longer, more sensuous romances filled with adventure, suspense, glamour and melodrama.

SIL-GEN-1RR

Available July 1986

Silhouette Desire

Texas Gold

The first in a great new
Desire trilogy by Joan Hohl.

In *Texas Gold* you can meet the
Sharp family—twins Thackery
and Zackery.

With Thackery, Barbara Holcomb,
New York model, embarks on an
adventure, as together they search for a
cache of stolen gold. For Barbara and
Thack, their gold is discovered in the
bright, rich vein of their love.

Then get to know Zackery and his half
sister Kit in *California Copper* and
Nevada Silver—coming soon from
Silhouette Books.

DT-1RA

COMING NEXT MONTH

THE GLORIOUS QUEST—Rita Rainville
When Kelly's mother and Jase's father ran off together, their
children chased after them, determined to bring them to their
senses—and promptly fell in love.

JURY OF HIS PEERS—Debbie Macomber
Wholesome, sincere Ted had always gotten on Caroline's nerves.
When they were both called for jury duty, temperatures in the
courtroom rose—and not from the court case!

SOMETHING SENTIMENTAL—Mia Maxam
Mallory was happy with her job as general manager of a small,
homey FM radio station—until the station was sold. Now she had
to contend with the new boss, Keith Alexander.

SWEPT AWAY—Donna McDowell
Jarod was everything Amanda wanted in a man, but he belonged
to another woman. Refusing to come between them, Amanda
tried to forget Jarod. But she had been swept away....

WHERE THERE'S A WILL—Joan Smith
Kathryn didn't mind when Joshua dragged her into a situation
straight out of a bad mystery novel. But when a man was as
dangerously handsome as Joshua, he could drag her anywhere!

GOOD TIME MAN—Emilie Richards
Jessica had dreamed of Alex Granger's kisses since she was
sixteen. But four years away at school hadn't prepared her for his
kind of loving—or leaving.

AVAILABLE THIS MONTH

UNHEAVENLY ANGEL
Annette Broadrick

MAGIC CITY
Lynnette Morland

AN IRRITATING MAN
Lass Small

MIRAGE
Mary O'Caragh

THE RIGHT MOVES
Arlene James

AMENDED DREAMS
Glenda Sands

Take 4 Silhouette Special Edition novels
FREE
and preview future books in your home for 15 days!

When you take advantage of this offer, you get 4 Silhouette Special Edition® novels FREE and without obligation. Then you'll also have the opportunity to preview 6 brand-new books —delivered right to your door for a FREE 15-day examination period—as soon as they are published.

When you decide to keep them, you pay just $1.95 each ($2.50 each in Canada) *with no shipping, handling, or other charges of any kind!*

Romance *is* alive, well and flourishing in the moving love stories of Silhouette Special Edition novels. They'll awaken your desires, enliven your senses, and leave you tingling all over with excitement... and the first 4 novels are yours to keep. You can cancel at any time.

As an added bonus, you'll also receive a FREE subscription to the Silhouette Books Newsletter as long as you remain a member. Each issue is filled with news on upcoming books, interviews with your favorite authors, even their favorite recipes.

To get your 4 FREE books, fill out and mail the coupon today!

Silhouette Special Edition®

Silhouette Books, 120 Brighton Rd., P.O. Box 5084, Clifton, NJ 07015-5084

Clip and mail to: Silhouette Books,
120 Brighton Road, P.O. Box 5084, Clifton, NJ 07015-5084 •

YES. Please send me 4 FREE Silhouette Special Edition novels. Unless you hear from me after I receive them, send me 6 new Silhouette Special Edition novels to preview each month. I understand you will bill me just $1.95 each, a total of $11.70 (in Canada, $2.50 each, a total of $15.00), with no shipping, handling, or other charges of any kind. There is no minimum number of books that I must buy, and I can cancel at any time. The first 4 books are mine to keep.

BS18R6

Name _____ (please print)

Address _____ Apt. #

City _____ State/Prov. _____ Zip/Postal Code

• In Canada, mail to: Silhouette Canadian Book Club, 320 Steelcase Rd., E.,
Markham, Ontario, L3R 2M1, Canada
Terms and prices subject to change.
SILHOUETTE SPECIAL EDITION is a service mark and registered trademark. SE-SUB-1

One of America's best-selling romance authors writes
her most thrilling novel!

TWIST OF FATE

JAYNE ANN KRENTZ

Hannah inherited the anthropological papers that could
bring her instant fame. But will she risk her life and give
up the man she loves to follow the family tradition?

Available in June at your favorite retail outlet, or reserve your copy for
May shipping by sending your name, address, and zip or postal code
along with a check or money order for $4.70 (includes 75¢ for postage
and handling) payable to Worldwide Library Reader Service to:

In the U.S.	In Canada
Worldwide Library	Worldwide Library
901 Fuhrmann Blvd.	P.O. Box 2800, 5170 Yonge St.
Buffalo, NY	Postal Station A, Willowdale, Ont.
14269	M2N 6J3

BPA—TOF-H-1

 WORLDWIDE LIBRARY®